Mind Games

First Edition

Alan DiLuca

Mind Games

First Edition

Published by The Nazca Plains Corporation
Las Vegas, Nevada
2006

ISBN: 978-1-887895-78-1

Published by

The Nazca Plains Corporation ®
4640 Paradise Rd, Suite 141
Las Vegas, NV 89109-8000

PUBLISHER'S NOTE
Mind Games is a work of fiction created wholly by *Alan DiLuca's*
imagination. All characters are fictional and any resemblance to
any persons living or deceased is purely by accident. No portion
of this book reflects any real person or events.

Editor, Blake Stephens

Dedication

For Dmitri, who sees the big picture.

Mind Games

Alan DiLuca

Contents

Being Neighborly

It's one of those things that happens in fiction, but never in real life. But the day the new neighbors moved in next door, life mirrored art. They were the quintessential All-American Couple, absolutely Stepford-perfect.

They were both blond, blue-eyed, and beautiful. Michelle, the wife, was about five foot three, in her early thirties, with a slim waist, a nice figure, and a nearly constant smile. But it was her husband Jim who really caught my eye. He stood a few inches over six feet tall with military-short hair, and under the grey Army T-shirt he was wearing as he lifted boxes, I could see hints of an incredible physique.

We didn't have much contact the first few years. Jim was a private person, and Michelle preferred to socialize with her women friends. But they had no problem living next door to our neighborhood's only gay couple, and we chatted every once in a while out in our driveways. During these chats, I learned that Jim used to be an Army Ranger, and served in both Guam and Germany. Now that he was out of the service, he still tried to stay in shape, lifting weights and running. Both he and his wife even ran marathons every once in a while.

The hints about his physique later proved to be dead-on accurate. I caught glimpses of him as he worked out in the yard. Disappointingly, he kept his shirt on more often than I wished. But he liked to wear short pants, and his legs were muscular and beautifully sculpted. And every once in a while, he would strip his shirt off as he walked to his garage after mowing his lawn and I got an eyeful of his sexy chest. He had classic washboard abs and giant slabs of pectoral muscle, crowned with half-dollar-sized nipples that practically begged my tongue to bathe them. His shoulders sat like cannonballs atop his back, and his arms were as big as my thighs.

There's one incident that I will never forget. It was one of the hottest days of summer, and I was cutting the grass. Jim came out dressed only in sneakers and a pair of tiny red shorts that clung like Saran wrap to his waist and butt. He started picking weeds out of his yard, and in a few minutes, his bare torso and back were gleaming with sweat. He kept bending over at the waist to pluck at the weeds. When I saw him standing there, ass in the air, it was all I could do to keep from running over and plugging him up right there in the hot sun. Usually I'm pretty conscientious about mowing in straight lines, but the zigzags and divots left in the yard after I was done made it pretty obvious my mind was elsewhere.

We stayed neighborly but distant until, coincidentally, Michelle became pregnant just as my husband and I were adopting our first child. The two kids were born only two months apart, and it was just natural that as they grew up, they started to play together. My husband and I both worked part-time, so we were each home with Taylor part of the week. Jim, on the other hand, had a full-time job, so it was mostly Michelle who we saw and got to know. Jim, like always, kept pretty much to himself.

Then, one day...

"Hey, Alex, how are you what's going on?" That's how he always said it - like the two questions were one sentence.

"Pretty good, Jim. How about you? You holding up OK with Michelle off at her folks'?" I answered. I was getting the mail. It was a Saturday in June, and the weather was hot and sticky. Jim was shirtless, and was out edging his driveway. I had happened to notice him from inside, and figured it was a good time to go get the mail. Not that I was spying on him or anything.

"Yeah, I'm good." He stopped, and we nodded at each other for a bit. He always seemed uncomfortable with casual conversation. I'm not much better at it, so I thought this would be the end of our talk. That was OK - I'd be content with a glimpse of his body from ten feet away. No need to be greedy and ask for a closer look. But then he surprised me and came over.

"Hey, do you have a minute?" he said.

"Sure, what's up?" His chest was now about two feet from mine. I tried to keep my eyes up, looking at his, but I couldn't stop my gaze from occasionally wandering downward. His chest, which always looked smooth from a distance, was actually fairly well covered with hair. He was so blond, though, that the hair blended into his skin when seen from farther away.

"You work with computers, right?" he said.

These days, pretty much everyone can say they "work with computers". But I write help-system authoring software for a living, so I guess it's truer of me than most people. "Yeah, I do," I answered.

"When you have some time, do you think you could take a look at my setup? I just ordered DSL service, and something's not right with it. I tried calling them, but they kept me on hold for 20 minutes and I gave up."

I had to revise my estimate of his nipples. They were at least the size of silver dollars. Usually I like guys with tiny, perky nipples, but for some reason, these giant man-tits were really turning me on.

"Sure, no problem, I'd be happy to. You want to do it now?". I couldn't believe the words coming out of my mouth. "You want to do it now?" Hell, I sure do!

Jim answered "You don't mind? It doesn't have to be right now, if you've got something going on."

"No, now's OK. Taylor is napping, and Noel's there in case he wakes up. Let's go take a look." Good God, the man's pecs were so well developed they cast shadows on his stomach!

I followed Jim in through the garage, intoxicated by the scent in the air behind him. We went upstairs to an extra bedroom where he had his computer. He gestured for me to take the driver's seat, and pulled up a chair for himself to the left of mine. Up close, his presence was overwhelming. His skin was still glistening with sweat, and the cool air in the house had caused his nipples to contract and harden, so they jutted temptingly out from his chest. His upper arm stretched in front of my lips as he reached for the mouse to wake the computer up.

Fortunately, the problem wasn't too hard to figure out - he had just confused a DNS with a proxy server when following the setup instructions. I was so drenched in his pheromones that I think I'd have had trouble solving anything more complex. Once we had tweaked a few settings, I went to bring up a web page to make sure it was working.

My fingers were about to type in Google's address, when I paused. "What the hell?" I thought, and typed in "www.ropejock. com" [* author's note: sadly now defunct]. The page came up right away, and with the high-speed connection, the front page image loaded almost instantly. It showed a man standing up, dressed in camouflage pants and naked from the waist up, with his arms tied back over his head to a frame and clips attached to his nipples.

As nonchalantly as I could, I said "yeah, it looks like everything's working. You should be good to go."

Jim was staring at the screen. "What's this site?" he asked.

"Oh, it's just a site I like to use to test internet connections. It's got a lot of pictures, so if they come up quickly, you know your high-speed connection is working okay. It looks like everything came up very fast - I think your new connection is working fine."

With that, I hit the back button but left the browser running. The display returned to the "404" message that had been showing when I sat down. Jim thanked me profusely and walked me to the door, but I could see he was still slightly distracted.

The seed was planted. Now I just had to wait.

The following Wednesday, I happened to be outside with Taylor when Jim came home from work. He came right over, not even stopping to get his mail.

"Hey, Alex, how are you what's going on?"

"I'm good, Jim. How's the DSL connection?"

"It works great. Thanks again for your help."

"Oh, you're welcome. No trouble at all." I found it a lot easier to be calm and collected near him when he was dressed. He was still a sexy hunk, though, and he looked mighty sharp in his business clothes.

Once again, the conversation froze, and I thought that would be the end. But then he looked down at Taylor drawing on the driveway, and I could tell he wanted to say something else but was worried about little pitchers with big ears. He started twice to speak, then stopped himself both times.

"Jim, he's two," I said, looking down at Taylor. "He speaks in two-word phrases. What did you want to say?"

"I just wanted to ask you about that web site," he blurted out.

"Ah," I said. "That web site. Okay. What do you want to know?"

"Well, I was wondering... Do you... Is that... What do you... Is that something you're... into?" he stammered.

"Some of it," I replied. "The main focus of Jack's site is tickling, which I'm not into at all. But he also has a lot of stuff with bondage and control, which I enjoy very much."

"Really? You mean you like to get tied up?"

"Yeah, I do. And I like to tie other guys up, too."

Taylor kept drawing, oblivious to a conversation I would never want him to hear when he was old enough to understand it.

"Wow. Is that something you and Noel do, then?"

"Sometimes. It's not really his thing, though. He knows I like bondage, and he indulges me from time to time, but we usually stick to what's enjoyable for us both."

"Oh," he said.

"But it's OK, because bondage doesn't have to be related to sex. Did you read any of the stories on Jack's web site?"

He looked a little abashed. "Some of them," he said.

"Then you know a lot of the guys who go to Jack's apartment are straight. It seems there are a lot of guys out there who are straight as arrows, but have this thing about being under someone else's control. They're not looking for sex, they just want to see how much they can take. It's a self-pride kind of thing. They let a guy tie them up and work them over a bit, and they get a kind of rush out of seeing how well they took the abuse."

I took another step closer to my hunky neighbor. "Tell me, Jim, why are you asking me this?"

He refused to meet my eyes. "Nothing, I was just curious..." His voice trailed off.

"Jim, is it because maybe you're curious how well YOU might do?"

"Well..."

"Did you maybe imagine yourself in some of those pictures?

"I thought..."

"Is that maybe why you're over here and we're having this conversation? Are you thinking maybe you and I might do a little... exploring?" I said.

Jim looked at the ground. "Well... it's something I've thought about. A little," he said. He finally met my gaze.

My heart leaped in my chest. He was hooked! I had him!

"All right," I said, "let me make you a proposition..."

———————————————————

"Hi, Michelle! Welcome home! You're back early." I called across the yards. She was home from her trip to see her parents in Atlanta. It was morning on a Tuesday - one of my stay-at-home-dad days - and Taylor and I were taking turns watering the garden. Michelle called something in reply, but I couldn't make out what she said.

She came over, with her little bundle of energy Joanne in tow. We made some small talk about her trip, and her parents, and the neighborhood, and the planes that always flew too low over our homes. Eventually, talk turned to the garden and the yard, which she constantly complimented Noel and me on. Some people would have started to sound insincere after so much repetition, but not Michelle - she genuinely was that sweet.

I told her that while she was gone, Noel and I had made a change to the landscaping in the yard. "Do you have a minute to take a look at something, Michelle? I want to make sure it's OK with you." I asked.

"Oh, of course it will be, Alex. You know I always like what you guys do here," she said.

I pointed over to the grape arbor I had put up on the far side of the garden and we walked over to it while the kids started piling rocks in Taylor's watering can. The structure was on our side of the property line, but just barely. Some of the grapes would probably eventually hang over into her yard, once the plants grew in.

"Take a look. I just want to make sure I'm not invading your turf. Is it OK with you if we do this here?"

"Alex, that is just fine by me," Michelle said. She was a very friendly, outgoing person, and her Southern accent came out a little more when she was feeling especially neighborly. "You know I have no problem with anything you guys want to do."

"Oh, I'm glad to hear that," I said. "I was worried it might bother you."

"Not at all, not at all. In fact, I kind of like it. And this is the perfect spot for it."

"Well, thanks. Hey, while you're here, take a look at these," I said, reaching into the garden and pulling on some tomatoes. Even though it was still early in the season, the weather had been hot, and we were already starting to get some ripe ones.

"Wow, now those are RED!" she said.

"Yeah, they're just about ready," I answered. Back on the driveway, Joanne had grown bored with the watering can and had wandered back over to her own yard. It looked like Taylor was itching to start spraying the hose again. Michelle said "Well, I'll let you two get back to work. Bye, now!"

"Bye, Michelle," I called after her. "By the way, help yourself to some tomatoes whenever you want - we can't possibly eat them all."

Just then, a plane appeared in the distance, starting its approach to the nearby airport. It was perfect timing - I was glad there had been none in the air as we were speaking, or it would have ruined the recording I was making of our conversation.

"You want me to go for a run?" Jim asked, somewhat incredulously.

"Right. Go get dressed in an old pair of shorts, something you don't care about. Socks, sneakers, no shirt. Then go for a run. I don't care how far. Five miles, maybe? Just go fast enough and far enough that you get hot, sweaty, and tired. Then come back. Oh, and before you go, bring over a change of clothes for afterward," I told him.

"Well, OK, but I don't get it."

"Here's the thing - your wife and daughter are at the beach, but my family will be home in a few hours. If we had a whole weekend, I'd start you off rested and relaxed, and work you up slowly. But we don't have the luxury of all that time, so I need to start you from a point where you're already physically tired. See?"

"Yeah, I guess that makes sense. OK, I'll go run. What do I do when I come back?"

"When you get back, come in right here, through the garage. I'll be waiting for you in the kitchen. At that time, I'll give you one more chance to back out. After that, if you decide to go ahead, you're committed to stay until I let you go, no matter what happens. Think about it while you're running. Once you commit, there's no turning back."

"OK," he said, and disappeared into his house to change. A few minutes later, he came back out and dropped a bundle of clothing in my garage. I watched him stretch a little, then head off down the street at a loping pace. He sure looked good with his shoulders gleaming in the hot August sun, and it would only get better when he returned, shining and dripping with sweat.

I went inside to wait. My heart was turning somersaults as I contemplated the afternoon ahead. Years of lusting fruitlessly after this guy were about to come to fulfillment.

Over the course of two weeks or so after our enlightening little chat back in June, Jim and I had worked out an arrangement. We agreed that the best time would be during vacation week in August. Jim couldn't get the full week off from work, but his wife and daughter were going to the beach, and he'd be going out to join them Thursday night. Thursday afternoon, Noel would be at work, and Taylor would be at my sister's house. I would take half a day off, Jim would take half a day off, and we'd see what we could do to fulfill his bondage fantasies in a completely non-sexual, non-heterosexual-masculinity-threatening way.

At least, that's what we talked about. My plans were a little different. I vaguely alluded to them as we were discussing the details.

"Now, Jim," I said, "this is going to be a non-sexual thing for you, but you know I'm gay, and I won't be able to help getting at least a little bit aroused at the situation. Is that OK with you? You won't freak out if start packing wood in my pants?"

"No, that's cool," he answered.

"OK," a pause. "I don't mean to push the point, but I do need to know what your limits are. See, one of the most effective ways to cause a man discomfort is through his genitals, and part of this scene will definitely involve me touching your cock and balls. I want to settle up front what's OK and what's not."

He was clearly uncomfortable discussing the subject. I pressed, and we eventually worked out that I could do whatever I wanted, but he was straight, and therefore 1) his mouth would not go anywhere near another man's dick, and 2) no dick was to go near his ass. I noticed that his limits did not preclude me giving him a hand job, or even a blow job, and there were some large loopholes in the "ass" portion of the contract, but I didn't call his attention to the fact. Caveat bondee, you know.

The other terms were easy - no permanent damage, no marks that he would have trouble explaining later that evening when he met up with his wife again. No blood, no exchange of body fluids. No problem. "And remember," I told him, "this isn't just about the bondage. I'm also going to try to mess with your mind. During the course of the scene, I might threaten to break one of these conditions we've set, but I won't actually do it unless you tell me it's OK."

I heard footsteps outside, and my mind snapped back to the present. The door to the garage opened, and Jim came in. He looked glorious. Sweat sheened his body from head to toe. His chest heaved up and down as he sucked air in and out. His holey shorts clung to his hips and left very little to the imagination as to what they covered. I stood up and offered him a glass of water, which he downed in one long pull. Then I held out a pair of handcuffs to my gorgeous neighbor.

"Decision time, Jim. If you want to proceed, put these on. If not, turn around and walk out, no hard feelings, and no one ever needs to know."

He hesitated only a moment before reaching out to take the cuffs.

"Not in front of you," I said as he started to lock them on his wrists. "Put your hands behind your back."

It was awkward for him, but he got the cuffs latched in place. I had him turn around so I could double-lock them to keep them from getting too tight. Close up, his sweaty man-scent was overpowering.

"Jim, from this point forward, feel free to fight me. I know you're here by your own free will, but as part of the scene, you can try to resist if you want to." Even though he was six inches taller than me and outweighed me by fifty pounds, I was pretty sure I could handle him as long as his hands stayed cuffed. Besides, he wouldn't be fighting too hard - we were neighbors, right?

"Sit down," I told him. He complied, hanging his arms over the back of the chair. I pulled out another pair of cuffs and locked the connecting chain of the first pair to the frame of the chair. Now he could stand up again, but he'd have to take the chair with him.

I went around it front of him and got right in his face. "YOU FUCKING ASSHOLE!" I shouted. He jumped in his chair - this was a surprise to him. "You are the BIGGEST GODDAMN PRICK-TEASE I've ever MET! For years you've been parading around outside in your skimpy little shorts, showing off your oh-so-sexy body, all the while knowing GODDAMN WELL I'm watching you, I'm wanting you, and I'm FUCKING HELPLESS to do a thing about it! Well, it is PAYBACK time, Jim-boy. Now YOU'RE the helpless one. You thought this was going to be just a little light bondage workout, but you, my friend, are in for a surprise."

He started to stammer something, but I cut him off.

"SHUT UP! The time has come to punish you for your bad behavior. You should have known better than to saunter around nearly naked like that. Those teeny little tight red shorts of yours look they're painted on, for God's sake! They leave NOTHING to the imagination! What did you think, you were doing me a favor or something, giving me a little peep show? Yeah, sure I liked watching you, but I need more than that, man. I need much more, I need the real thing. You can't just tease me like that and expect to get away with it. There are CONSEQUENCES for your actions,

Jim, CONSEQUENCES that need to be paid!"

By this time, the sweat dripping off his face was mixed with my spit. He had a fearful look in his eyes, like he couldn't quite figure out what was going on. Was I "messing with his head" like I told him I would, or was he in over his head for real? I watched him test the cuffs holding his hands together. There was, of course, no give.

I reached over for a black leather hood as I muttered to myself. "Goddamn cock-teasing son of a bitch. You're gonna be begging me for mercy, you asshole." The hood had eyeholes (currently covered), a hole at the nose for breathing, and an opening at the mouth that could be plugged with a gag.

He thrashed a little in the chair, but I was able to hold him still long enough to work the hood down over his head and start lacing it down the back. The slick sweat made it that much easier to slide the leather over his skin. Once his world went dark, he started to protest "Hey, Alex, I didn't..."

"YOU SHUT THE FUCK UP!" I cut him off. He jumped again, and closed his mouth. I moved right next to his ear, this time speaking softly and slowly. "Don't you dare speak again without my permission, you worthless little toad. I know ways of causing you all kinds of pain, pain that doesn't leave marks. If you make me angrier than I already am, I will show you every single one of those ways, and there will be nothing you can do about it, now or afterward. You can feel free to go to the cops, but it'll be your word against mine, because there won't be a shred of physical evidence to back up your story. But you want to be very careful about going public, Jimmy, unless you're absolutely certain how Michelle will react when she learns about your little adventure with the gay boy next door. You have gotten yourself in over your head, my friend. You're swimming in the deep water now."

He held still while I finished tightening the laces of the hood. Then I stuffed a gag in his mouth, forcing it between his teeth and snapping it into place on the hood. For extra measure, I pressed hard with my hand, sealing the leather up against the skin around his mouth. Immediately, air started whistling through the nose holes as Jim, still breathing hard from his run, tried to get air in and out of his lungs.

"You like that, Jim? You like trying to catch your breath through that tiny hole?" He shook his head. I continued to hold tight, watching his struggles grow more frantic.

After about thirty seconds I let up the pressure and said "All right, but if you say another word, this gag's going right back in. Behave yourself." I unsnapped the gag and pulled it out of his mouth. Jim gasped gratefully at the life-giving air.

While Jim recovered, I removed his socks and shoes and locked a chain around his ankles, with about twelve inches of play between his feet. Then I locked another chain around his neck, with three feet of leader hanging out from the front, so that he was leashed like a dog. The chain was wrapped with plastic padding in the area where it made contact with his neck. Finally, I unclipped the cuffs attaching his wrists to the chair and told him to get up, pulling on his leash for good measure.

He did, awkwardly, rising to his feet while disentangling his arms from behind the chair. Before he could stand completely, I gave his neck chain a savage jerk downward and shouted "Not on your feet, moron! Down on your knees!"

Jim crashed heavily to his knees, brought down by the yank on the chain and his own misbalance. He let out a short yelp of pain, then quickly muffled it, fearing what punishment I might inflict on him for speaking. This was going very well, indeed. I told him "You are to remain on your knees at all times unless I tell you otherwise." Jim's hooded head nodded, unprompted. The manly, sweaty scent of his body began to be tinged with the smell of fear.

"Now, move forward," I ordered. He obediently shuffled forward, one knee and then the other, while I provided forward pressure using the chain. I guided him over to the top of the stairs that led down to the basement, then turned him so he was facing away from the steps.

"You're going to go backward down seven steps, on your knees. Be careful. I don't want to have to drag you back upright with this chain if you fall over." It took him almost two minutes, but he managed it, sliding carefully back, touching the next step down with his toes, and easing his knees down to the next step. With no hands for balance or eyes for guidance, it was a pretty tricky feat.

When he reached the landing, I backed him around the 180-degree turn, then had him go down six more steps to the basement. The floor was concrete; no problem for now, but in time it would come to feel like hot coals to poor Jim's knees. I turned him around and half-dragged him over to a twin-size bed, made up with a fitted sheet but nothing else. I let him shuffle forward until his chest bumped into foot end of the mattress.

"Up, Jim," I said, yanking the chain upward. "Sit up on the bed." He rose awkwardly, until he was high enough to turn around and rest his butt on the mattress. His chained feet rested on the floor near one of the legs of the bed. I tied a rope around one ankle and fastened it to the bed leg. Then I tied a longer rope to connect his other ankle to the farther bed leg. The ropes were tight enough to stretch his legs out to the full 12-inch separation that the connecting chain allowed, but once the chain came off, there would be plenty of slack. That was OK - this initial tie-down was just to keep him under control while I transferred him from the handcuffs to the bed. I would tighten him up later.

Next I fastened long ropes from his wrists to the corners of the headboard. Once they were in place, I undid the handcuffs. Gradually, I started pulling the ropes tighter, first one, then the other, undoing the knot, pulling out some slack, and tying it fast again. Jim caught on to what I was doing after the second repetition and tried to slide his hands around in front of him to pick at the knots around his wrists. He was, of course, stopped short - the four feet or so of play that the ropes allowed him was not enough to let him get his hands in front of his body. So he tried to slide backward along the mattress, but his leg ropes prevented too much backward movement, and I pulled some more slack out of the arm ropes as he went. He next tried to pick at the knots with his wrists still behind his back, but I kept pulling the lines tighter and tighter, messing up his work.

I kept it up for a little while, reeling him in like a fish. It wasn't long before he didn't have enough slack to stay sitting up, and fell over onto his back. At that point, his wrists got pulled up above his head, and he pretty much lost any hope of setting himself free, since he couldn't reach one hand with the other.

Once he realized he was completely helpless, I took my time stretching him out. I released the chain joining his legs together, then did to his ankles what I had done to his wrists, gradually pulling them to the corners of the bed. I got him centered on the bed by yanking hard in the direction I needed him to go until he shimmied over to where I wanted him, then tying the rope down again.

At last he was perfectly positioned. His muscular body lay face-up on the twin-size bed, with his limbs stretched tightly out to the four corners. At this point I replaced the ropes with more permanent ones - he was going to be in this position for a while, and I didn't want to leave marks on his skin. So I forced heavy ski mittens down over his hands and tied new ropes over them, snugging them tightly on his wrists so he had no chance of wiggling free. Then I tied these new ropes even more tightly to the bed, stretching his taut limbs even harder. I did the same to his ankles, using strips of cloth as padding.

Next, I strapped him down at the knees and elbows, again using cloth to protect his skin from the rope. I tied a long rope to one elbow, passed it under the bed and up the other side, and tied it tightly to his other elbow. His knees got the same treatment.

When I was finished, my handsome, studly, muscular neighbor was completely immobilized, wearing nothing but torn grey Army shorts and a hood. The only part of his body he could move was his head, and that didn't do him much good since it was completely encased in leather.

I sat down on the bed next to his chest and slapped my hand a few times on one meaty pectoral muscle. "Damn, you look good all trussed up like that," I said. I allowed my hand to trail down his stomach toward the waistband of his shorts. "I'm really looking forward to seeing the whole package, you know? But there's no rush - we've got plenty of time." Jim tried to flinch away from my fingers, which were snapping the elastic against his taut skin, but there was nowhere he could go.

"Now, Jim, I'm going to leave you here a while so you can think about the situation you've gotten yourself into. But before I do, I need to put the gag back in your mouth. You can either co-operate with me, or resist. If you co-operate, it'll go in easy, and all will be well. If you resist, the gag will still eventually go in your mouth, but you'll cause yourself a lot of unnecessary... discomfort... in the process. You choose, but choose now, because here it comes."

He chose to co-operate. The gag slid smoothly into his mouth. It was about two inches of hard rubber, quite thick, and shaped like the tip of a penis. I snapped it into place on the hood - Jim would not be doing much talking until I decided to let him. Air moved in and out of the hood's nose holes, much more smoothly than before - he was recovering from the exertion of his run.

"Bye, Jimmy. I'll be back in a little while," I called. I didn't actually leave, but instead settled myself into a chair by the door. I knew he wouldn't be able to hear the little noises I would make because the hood muffled and distorted sound.

The next fifteen minutes were a very enjoyable show. Jim was an athletic guy, and athletic guys don't do very well when they're forced into immobility. All those muscles were built to move, and they're not very happy when they can't. I watched as his discomfort grew. It started with little twitches in his feet, or along his ribs. Soon he was contorting his body as much as his restraints would allow, pointing his toes or arching his back; pulling hard on one arm to try to give the other some relief from the strain; lifting his head and thrashing it from side to side, as though trying to somehow dislodge the locked-on hood. He was not in any actual pain, but he was obviously suffering quite a bit of discomfort.

As I said, it was a very enjoyable show. I sat back and watched, stroking my cock as I appreciated each oh-so-limited movement he made. At last, he stopped struggling for several minutes. I judged that he had zoned out - his mind was elsewhere, thinking about something other than his physical condition. It was time for me to make a re-entrance.

I crept silently up to the side of the bed, and began to run my fingers along his leg, just brushing the hairs along the inside of his left calf. It took a few seconds before he noticed me, but when he did, he jumped like he had been hit by a bolt of lightning. I continued to touch him, gradually working my way upward along his leg until I was tickling the skin of his inner thigh, right at the bottom hem of his shorts. He squirmed the whole way, but there was nothing he could do about it.

While my one hand continued to play with the skin and cloth near his crotch, I used my other hand to lay a knife across his belly. I left it there for him to ponder while my strokes came closer and closer to his cock, outlined nicely against the fabric of his shorts. At last I touched it through the cloth, eliciting another twitch from my bound victim. I stroked it for a while, feeling it slowly grow stiff. I don't care how "straight" a guy is - when his cock gets attention, it's going to respond, no matter how much its owner wishes it wouldn't.

When he was about at half mast, I picked the knife up off Jim's belly and began rubbing the dull edge along the fabric covering his shaft. He moaned into his gag and his helpless thrashings grew more intense while his cock continued to stiffen. I didn't neglect his balls, either, reaching under his shorts to roll them around in my palm.

After several minutes of genital massage, Jim was completely hard. I grabbed the cloth and bunched it up in my fist. Then I sliced through it with the knife, making sure that the steel made plenty of contact with various parts of his groin. I was very careful not to touch him with the sharp edge, but there was no way he could know that with his head encased by the hood. He yelled and hollered and thrashed around each time the blade touched him. It took some sawing to cut through both legs of his shorts, especially with him flailing around as he was. When I was done, I yanked the remaining shreds of fabric out from under his ass and took my first good close look at the package I had been admiring from a distance for so long.

He didn't disappoint. His cock was a good seven inches long, and beautifully proportioned. It curved upward with perfect symmetry and ended in a flawless mushroom-cap head. His balls were thick and meaty, and hung like eggs between his splayed legs. I leaned down, burying my nose in his ball sac and taking a good long whiff, loud enough for him to hear it. He moaned in disgust - the words were probably supposed to be something like "aw, you sick fuck", but they came out mostly mmms and fffs.

"What's that, Jim? You want a whiff, too? Okay..." I grabbed one shred of his discarded shorts and rubbed it good and hard in the sweat between his balls and his legs. Then I taped it over the the nose holes of the hood. Any air that went in or out would have to pass through the sweat-soaked cloth. "There you go, Jim. Now you can enjoy it, too."

I strapped a leather ring around the base of his genitals, to encourage him to stay hard. Then I left him alone again for another fifteen minutes or so.

He squirmed some more, totally unable to get comfortable. This time, every movement of his body set his flagpole of a cock wiggling in the air. Once again I enjoyed the show. To think this gorgeous hunk of bondage-hungry man-meat had been right next door. What a shame for all the wasted time...

Finally, he settled down again, floating off with his mind in some other place. His cock had softened a bit, too, although it was still semi-solid. I crept up quietly to stand beside him, and whacked his balls with a ruler.

He would have hit the roof if he could, and I know the muffled grunts coming out though his gag were not words fit for our kids to hear. I hadn't really hit his nuts very hard, but the wooden ruler makes a very satisfying "crack" as it lands, and it had caught him completely by surprise.

"All right, you lazy bum, nap time's over. Get up, come on, let's go! Move, move, move!" I shouted at him, punctuating each word with another smack to his balls. He squirmed and fought to get away from the pounding assault, but there was no escape. "You retard, what's the problem? I told you to get up. Up, up, up! Let's go." I grabbed the chain attached to his neck and tugged him upward, still pounding on his balls. "UP!" His head and shoulders left the bed as I pulled, but the tight ropes prevented him from moving any farther. He was shouting into the gag.

I finally let up on the pounding and let go of the neck chain. Jim's head dropped back down onto the bed. "All right," I said, "since you are such a worthless wretch that you can't even follow simple instructions, I think it's time for some attitude adjustment lessons."

With that, I reversed the process I had used to get him down onto the bed, easing the tension in his arm ropes until I could get his hands cuffed behind him again, then releasing the leg ropes and chaining his ankles together, all the while making sure he stayed under my control.

With Jim on his knees again, I led him by the neck over to another area of the basement, where there was a short length of chain hanging down from one of the rafters, midway between two of the support poles that held up the house. I stood up on a chair and told Jim to stand up, tugging upward as I did. He climbed carefully to his feet, and when he was steady, I clipped his neck chain to the one hanging from the ceiling. There was enough slack that he could lower himself two or three inches before being stopped by the steel noose.

Next I removed the chain connecting his ankles and then fastened ropes from his legs to the support poles on either side. I pulled on his ankles until they were not quite a yard apart, then tied off the ropes. This had the effect of lowering Jim's torso until all the slack was gone from his neck chain. It wasn't hurting him, but he was unable to bend at the waist or the knees without being stopped short by the chain.

With his legs spread wide, and no way for him to bend over, his cock and balls hung open and vulnerable, in the perfect position for me to set to work on them. I started by fondling them and caressing them until his erection was straining fully upward again. Then I started kneading a little harder, squeezing his balls until I was rewarded with muffled grunting sounds leaking from around the gag. Jim tried to pull away from my hard-working hands, but there was nowhere for him to go, and no way for him to get his own hands around front.

Finally, I stretched his balls out, pulling them down in their sac, and fastened a parachute stretcher around them. I also taped on two electrical leads, one on each side of his sac, each wire nestled right up against a trapped testicle. The wires ran down and over to a control box sitting on a nearby table. With the hood on, Jim didn't know what I had done, but he would find out soon enough when the current started flowing.

Jim's hands were next. I had a pair of ten-pound free weights handy. One at a time, I wrapped his fingers around the handle, then used several feet of duct tape to ensure that he couldn't let go of the weights. With his hands still cuffed behind his back, I ran ropes from the weights up to pulleys fixed to the rafters. The pulleys were located right above where his hands would be if he stretched them out straight to the sides. From there the ropes ran down to a single hook in the floor, located right between his feet.

I stood behind Jim and pulled upward on the free ends of the ropes. The force transmitted through the pulleys yanked his hands upward behind his back, until they were pulled painfully up between his shoulder blades. Then I released the cuffs. Before he could react, I pulled even harder. He squirmed, and was able to untwist his arms out to the sides. I kept reeling in the slack until his arms were stretched up over his head in a Y shape, and then I stepped on the rope to keep him that way.

I attached the free ends of the ropes to the parachute stretcher on his balls, estimating how much slack to leave. When they were hooked fast, I took my foot off the ropes. Jim was now able to lower his arms, but he quickly discovered that if he brought them down below his nipples, he would get a strong tug on his trapped nuts. He decided to settle the weights on his shoulders, arms curled as though striking a body-building pose.

Still behind him, I started running my fingers over the skin of his sides, back, and shoulders, then kneading the muscles beneath. He was about as tense as a man can get, with sweat beading the hairs of his armpits and trickling down his neck from under the hood. He very obviously wanted me to stop touching him, and was trying to pull away from my hands. To drive home his feelings of helplessness, I pressed my body up against him, so that his ass could feel my rock-hard cock straining through the fabric of my shorts. I ground against him a few times while he shuddered in his bonds.

I reached around his head, unzipped the hood's mouth, and removed the gag so that he could breathe freely for what was coming next. He started to speak, but I reached down and squeezed his balls. "Shut. Up." I said in his ear. He did. "What did I tell you about speaking?" I continued. "If you want that gag back in your mouth, by all means, keep talking."

After a long enough pause to make sure he stayed still, I released his balls and went on. "Jim, it's time for you to get to work. Here is what is going to happen. You're into exercise and working out, right? You like to keep that body looking so hot and so sexy. Well, you're going to work out for me now.

"You are currently holding ten pounds in each hand. You are going to stretch your arms out to your sides so that they are parallel with the floor. You are going to keep your arms nice and straight as you slowly lift them up over your head, pause, then slowly lower them back down until they are parallel again. This will be one rep. You will then pause, and begin again. After each rep, you will call out the number of the rep you have just finished.

"You will maintain perfect form throughout. Your arms will remain perfectly straight. Your movements will be slow and smooth. If you falter in any way, you will be punished. If you stop, you will be punished.

"If you need me to explain any of this again, say 'I don't understand'. If you understand what I have said, say 'I understand'."

Jim swallowed and said "I understand."

"You will do 200 reps. Begin."

Jim paused only a fraction of a second before his hands were on the move. Out to his sides, then slowly up, slowly down. "One." Up, down. "Two." Up, down. "Three."

I admired the play of muscles from behind, then wandered around to take in the front view. So far, his form was perfect. The muscles in his chest and shoulders bulged and writhed like snakes as he raised and lowered the weights. "Twenty-three." "Twenty-four."

His breathing grew faster and heavier. Up, down. "Forty-six." Up, down. "Forty-seven." The motion was not quite as smooth as when he started, but still acceptable.

In the sixties, his form started to crack. His elbows began to bend a bit, and his moves had been getting faster and more jerky. "This is your only warning, Jim. Keep your arms straight, move slowly and smoothly, or you will be punished."

Fear drove him to shape up for a few more reps. Sweat was dripping down his body. He made it to seventy-one, then paused too long in the "up" position. I pressed a button on the control box. Current shot down the wires and through his balls.

Jim grunted as though he had been punched in the gut. He tried to double over and would have dropped the weights if he could, but he could do neither. "OH, SHIT!" he screamed, then compounded his pain by trying to lower his arms, giving his balls a powerful tug. "OH, MY GOD, MY BALLS!"

"HEY!" I shouted. "Shut up and get back to work, or I'll turn this knob up a notch and zap you again. You want that?"

He pulled himself together and started lifting again. Once again fear and adrenalin drove him on, but the muscles in his arms were nearing exhaustion. After five more reps, his arms were shaking uncontrollably. After another three, there was just no way he could keep lifting the weights; his arms simply couldn't do it.

Zap. "AAARRRGH!"

"LIFT, DAMN YOU!" I screamed from behind him. "MOVE YOUR GODDAMN ARMS!" Jim's chest was heaving as he struggled to lift the weights again. He had lost count, and his form was completely shot.

Zap. "AAAAIIIIGGGH, FUCK!"

"GET YOUR ARMS MOVING, OR SO HELP ME I'LL MASH MY FINGER DOWN ON THIS BUTTON AND NEVER LET UP."

Jim started begging for me to stop. I kept shouting at him, until at last it was clear that his exhausted muscles had hit their absolute limit. He rested the weights on his shoulders again, and grimaced through the pain of two more shocks while trying to hold back sobs.

"Fine," I told him, finally releasing the button. "Some he-man you turned out to be. I really expected better, you pathetic little wuss. You have no willpower at all. So you know what? Since you don't have the mental strength to make your muscles do the work, I guess I'll just have to supply the willpower for you..."

I pulled out two more ropes and tied one to each of the weights. Then I looped them around two of the support poles in the basement, one on each side of him. One at a time, I pulled the ropes tight and tied them off. Now Jim was forced to hold his weighted arms out straight at his sides, parallel to the floor, each hand supporting a ten-pound weight. Breath hissed out of his mouth and he began to softly say "Oh God... Oh God...".

His muscles were so spent that they couldn't help him at all, so the full force of the twenty pounds was effectively hanging from his balls. The parachute harness stretched them out from his body, down toward the floor. They looked luscious hanging there, the taut skin engorged with blood. I dropped to my knees and began to run my tongue across the shiny surface. I was rewarded with a deep moan from Jim, and his cock, which had softened during his workout, rose quickly to full mast again, helped by the leather ring that still encircled the base.

I shifted my attention to his penis, nibbling at the head and coating it with my spit. Tentative licks gave way to a full-throated blow job as Jim struggled with the conflicting sensations of pleasure and pain. I gave him my best, alternating deep plunges with light licks to the sensitive underside of the head. I was in heaven, and, despite the condition he was in, Jim was clearly enjoying it, too. After ten minutes or so, I could tell by the increased swelling against my tongue that he was very nearly ready to shoot his load. I abruptly pulled away.

"Not so fast, Jimbo." He moaned in frustration and pumped his hips into the empty air - gently, of course, so as not to further stretch his balls. They had turned a beautiful shade of deep purple.

"You'll remember, of course, that the whole point of this little exercise is to see how much you can take. Well, now that you're warmed up, we can get started. It's time to play a little game, Jim."

"Alex, wait, no, I gotta stop." Something in his voice told me he was serious. I quickly untied the arm ropes and helped him move the weights to rest on his shoulders, then detached the ropes from his ball stretcher. He was able to stand in a sort of "parade rest" posture. I went behind him and spoke reassuringly into his ear, rubbing his back gently.

"Jim, it's OK, it's OK. You're doing great, Jim. You can do this."

"No, I... I think I'm done. This was... definitely more than I was expecting."

"But you're taking it like a man, Jim." I soothed him some more. "Tell you what, why don't we take a little break? Then, if you want to call it quits after that, fine - we'll quit. But I think you can see this through to the end. In fact, I'm sure you can. You must have taken more punishment than this in your Army Ranger days, right? I know you can handle anything I can give you. I'm just messing with your mind like I said I would."

He agreed to reconsider after a break. I untaped the weights from his wrists, gave him some slack in his ankles, detached the neck chain from the ceiling, and unsnapped the blindfold, removing it from the hood. He rested, standing, while we chatted about inconsequential stuff - his work, the kids, his upcoming beach vacation, and so on. I tried to give him some feeling of normalcy, something to remind him that, even though he was chained up, naked and hooded, in the basement of his homosexual neighbor, he hadn't completely given up on his real life.

Being able to see helped, I'm sure. Until I took the blindfold off, he had been in total darkness since shortly after walking into my kitchen. I think having his vision restored, even temporarily, took away a lot of his disorientation. After all, it was just my basement. There was a baby swing that Taylor had outgrown sitting not ten feet away, for Pete's sake. How scary could it be?

After a while, I walked over in front of him and stared through the tiny holes into his very blue eyes. "I'm going to put the blindfold back on now. Is that OK?" After a long pause, he nodded, and then the darkness closed in on him again.

I retied him so that his hands were attached to the ceiling instead of his balls. He stood with his arms and legs spread wide, his body making a well-muscled X. I stretched him out very tightly so that he had to stand up on his toes. It was a position that would quickly grow uncomfortable, then painful, as the muscles in his legs, which were already tired out from his run, grew increasingly unable to support his weight. Before too long, he would have to start spending time hanging from his wrists, and from then on his predicament would only get worse. I left the gag out of his mouth.

"Well, Jim, I told you we were going to play a little game. The game is called 'Tough Guy Trivial Pursuit'. Remember that time last winter when you and Michelle had us over for dinner and we played Trivial Pursuit afterwards? I got the feeling then that you weren't exactly using all your brainpower. Maybe it was the vodka tonic. Or the distraction of the kids. Whatever the reason, it doesn't matter, because I've thought of a way to inspire you to put your mind in high gear. Here's how the game works..."

I explained the rules to him as I made arrangements around him. I tied a rope to the leader of his neck chain and ran it through a pulley over his head, then to a second pulley some feet away, leaving the free end hanging down. I tied a bucket to the end of the rope, and hung a second smaller bucket from the parachute harness around his balls.

"I'm hooking you up to a neck bucket and a ball bucket. The buckets will contain weights. Each time you get a question right, I take weight out of one of the buckets. When you get a question wrong, I put weight into one of the buckets. You get to choose which bucket, but you have to choose before you hear the question. You also get to choose the category, but you have to answer all six questions on one card before we go on to the next. Simple, really.

"The neck bucket goes in increments of five pounds, and the ball bucket goes one pound at a time. If you manage to empty both buckets, you win, and as a prize, I'll let you inflict any revenge on me that you want. But if you get up to ten weights in each bucket, I win. I'll decide what my prize is later.

"We're going to start out with ten pounds in your neck bucket, and two pounds in your ball bucket. All you have to do is get four questions right, and you win right off the bat. Easy enough, huh?"

I took two 5-lb and two 1-lb weights and put them in place. Jim barely noticed the neck weight, but the two pounds on his balls seemed to make him wince. He tried to thrust his hips backward to set his pelvis at a better angle to take the weight. It was hard to do, while still maintaining his balance on his toes.

"Question 1: neck or balls, Jim?" I said.

"Uh, neck," he replied.

"And what category do you want first?"

"Sports." How predictable.

"OK, Sports and Leisure it is. What's the first instruction given runners by the starter of a race?"

He didn't pause long before giving his answer. "On your marks?"

"Correct," I said. "As promised, one five-pound neck weight comes out. Very good, Jim-boy. Want to try for a ball weight, now?"

"Yeah. Geography."

"Geography: What Italian landmark has 296 steps?"

This one stumped him. He hemmed and hawed for a while. I told him that if he didn't answer the questions in a timely fashion, I'd have to reattach the ball zapper and institute a time limit. He guessed pretty quickly after that. "The Colosseum?"

"Nope. The Leaning Tower of Pisa. Sorry." I added another pound to the ball bucket. He didn't like that.

"What's next? Think about this, Jim - if you get one more weight off your neck, you're halfway to winning, because once the bucket is empty, you never have to choose 'neck' again. Want to try for it?"

He did, and chose Entertainment.

"Who was known as America's Favorite Flying Cowboy?"

He had no idea. Five pounds of neck weight went back in.

He was able to get the Science question right (yellow fever is transmitted by mosquitoes), but he blew both History and Arts and Leisure for a total of two right, four wrong. After the first card, he had three pounds hanging from his balls and fifteen pulling at his neck. He broke even on the second card, redistributing the weight to four balls, ten neck. His legs were starting to quiver.

After that, things went downhill. He got only one answer right on the third card, leaving him at five and twenty-five. The weights were starting to bother him. He kept squirming around, testing the limits of his mobility in an effort to find some relief. There was none to be found. Every time he inched his neck upward to ease the pressure, the bucket dropped lower and brought the full weight back down on him again. So to get back to "normal", he would have to make a concerted effort to pull himself back down as much as possible, yanking the neck bucket back up, only to start all over again. And every movement he made set the ball bucket swinging around, tugging on his nuts from all sides. I was in my glory watching him.

When the score was 7 balls, 30 neck, there came the sound of the doorbell ringing upstairs. I told Jim we'd have to take a break.

"Now, I can't have you making any noise down here, so I'm going to put the gag back in. But I want you to be able to breathe, so I'm going to unhook the neck bucket from the rope. Now don't go anywhere... I'll be right back.

I can only imagine the thoughts that went through Jim's head as I left him alone in the basement. He was utterly helpless. His body was stretched from floor to ceiling, arms and legs splayed to expose his nakedness. Seven pounds of weight dangled from his balls. The black leather hood on his head blocked all light from his eyes. He couldn't speak with the gag in his mouth, not that he could necessarily have thought of anything to say, anyway.

Through the muffling leather of the hood, he would have heard me climbing the stairs and answering the door. He could probably hear voices as I spoke to the visitor, but would not have been able to make out words or even identify who the visitor was.

His heart would have started racing wildly when he heard not one, but two sets of footsteps coming down the stairs. He would have fought with all his might in a useless effort to break free of the bondage I had put him in.

And I think he nearly pissed himself when he heard me say from the foot of the stairs, just around the corner from where his trapped and helpless body stood, "Do you have a minute to take a look at something, Michelle? I want to make sure it's OK with you."

Michelle's voice responded, "Oh, of course it will be, Alex. You know I always like what you guys do here."

Me: "Take a look. I just want to make sure I'm not invading your turf. Is it OK with you if we do this here?"

Michelle: "Alex, that is just fine by me. You know I have no problem with anything you guys want to do."

Me: "Oh, I'm glad to hear that. I was worried it might bother you."

Michelle: "Not at all, not at all. In fact, I kind of like it. And this is the perfect spot for it."

Me: "Well, thanks." Jim would have felt my hand grabbing his balls, lifting them forward and upward, then heard my voice again. "Hey, while you're here, take a look at these."

"Wow, now those are RED!" came Michelle's voice.

"Yeah, they're just about ready."

Then a long, uncomfortable pause before Michelle's voice came one more time. "Well, I'll let you two get back to work. Bye, now!" Footsteps sounded on the stairs again, two sets going up. More voices at the door, then one set of feet coming back down.

When I got back downstairs, Jim was breathing shallowly. His leg muscles kept shaking in periodic spasms. I pulled the gag out of his mouth.

"You heard the lady, Jim. She has no problem with anything 'us guys' want to do. That's good to know, because I'm getting a little tired of this game. You don't seem to know the answers to very many of these questions, and frankly, it's a bit boring just tossing in the weights one after another."

I continued "So I'll tell you what. I'll give you a choice. We can either plow ahead and you can get to the end that we both know is coming one weight at a time, or you can bet it all on one question. If you get it right, you win. If not, I win. What do you say?"

"OK."

"'OK' what? OK to one question? Say 'yes' if you're sure."

"Yes. One question."

I said "All righty, then. Here's your one question. Get it right, and you're a free man. Get it wrong, and I'll have to exercise my creative mind and come up with an appropriate reward for myself. Here goes..."

"V kakoi yazik ya seichas' govoryu?"

There was a brief pause, then Jim burst out with "Aw, what the hell is that, German? That's not a fair ques- ooof!" My fist crashing into his stomach cut short his protests and set the seven pounds swinging widely between his legs.

"Sorry, Jim, 'German' is not correct. The answer to the question 'In what language am I now speaking?' is 'Russian', or, if you want the full version, 'ti govorish' po-russki.' Sorry, but you lose."

The gag went back in when he opened his mouth to complain again, turning his complaints into muffled hissing noises. I walked around behind him and spoke into his ear.

"You'll be pleased to know that I won't keep you in suspense; I've already decided what my prize is." I held up a seven-inch-long, one-inch-diameter dildo and rolled it against his chest. With my other hand I began to tickle the skin of his ass, circling steadily closer to his tightly-clenched sphincter. "Feel this, Jim? For my reward, I get to put this nice, thick, plastic cock right... inside... of... you." On the last word, my thumb made contact with his hole and I gave it a poke.

He yelped into the gag and lurched forward as far as the ropes would allow. His legs gave out completely for a moment, and he hung by his wrists until he could get them back under control. He started speaking more muffled words, but I cut him off.

"What's that, Jim? That's against the rules that we set, you claim? Ah, but it's not. See, the rules say that your mouth does not go anywhere near another man's dick, and that no dick is to go near your ass. Well, this isn't a dick. It's a dildo. Perfectly legal. If you were concerned about dildos going up your ass, you should have thought of that when we were deciding on the rules. It's far too late now to change your mind. I just need to get both you and your latex lover here greased up and we can begin."

I slathered lube all over the dildo, then coated Jim's ass with a generous helping. He was visibly torn between apprehension and stoicism as my hand rubbed the cream between his spread cheeks, my finger occasionally poking at his opening.

"Now, I'm assuming that, straight hunk that you are, you've never had anything up your ass before. Am I wrong? Tell me if I'm wrong, because I'm about to give you advice on how to handle your first anal invasion, and I'll sound pretty silly if you're actually an old pro at this. Nod yes if this is your first butt-fucking."

He swallowed, and nodded his head.

"OK, what you want to do is loosen up. Pretend like you're pushing something out, and it'll make it much easier for me to push this in. If you tighten your sphincter, the process will cause you a lot more discomfort. Bear in mind, it's going in one way or another, so whether you cooperate or not makes no difference to me. But to you, it can make a lot of difference. So ask yourself - how much pain do I want?"

I rubbed the plastic cock against his greased hole, sliding it up, down, and around. I teased him by repeatedly pressing it in, only to stop before actually penetrating him. Finally, he was so desperate to get it over with that he seemed actually hungry for it. That was my cue.

"OK, Jim, it's time. Open up and push." He did. I pressed the plastic dick hard against his hole, and bit by bit, it began to slip inside. Jim inhaled as the tender tissue of his ass stretched to accommodate the invader. I slowly, slowly, drove it in further, until it slipped past the sphincter and progress suddenly became much easier. The whole seven inch length was soon buried deep, with only the base protruding out.

I wrapped a rope around his stomach, and looped another over it in the front. The second rope ran down between his legs, one strand on either side of his genitals. The two strands joined up again between his ass cheeks, flush up against the dildo, and I tied the free ends to the stomach rope in the back. The ropes made a sort of jock strap, holding the dildo firmly in place.

I moved around to the front and admired my captive. He was a splendid sight: trussed up like an X, hooded, blinded, gagged, ass-plugged, and with seven pounds of weight hanging from his very purple balls. His entire body was drenched with sweat from the ordeal of fighting the bondage, and it was clear that he would not have the endurance to continue the fight very much longer. He was moaning softly with every breath he took. His cock, despite the leather ring that still encircled the base, was completely soft.

Unlike mine.

After a good, long look, I stepped forward and began to play with his body. I stroked, rubbed, brushed, and licked him, from his leather-encased head to his straining legs. I worshipped his beautiful muscles, experiencing in one burst what I had fantasized about for five years.

He responded. Despite the discomfort of his position, and despite any lingering doubts he may have had, his nipples perked under my tongue and his gorgeous cock swelled until it was pointing straight out. I paid all three sensitive spots all the careful, warm, wet attention they deserved, and periodically tugged and jiggled the plug in his ass just to remind him it was there.

Time crawled by - it could have been minutes or hours. I had no idea.

Finally, I felt Jim's cock start to swell against my tongue. His breathing quickened, and started to come in isolated gasps. I stopped sucking him before he could reach his climax, and he nearly exploded in despair when he realized he couldn't quite make it over the edge.

I stood up and whispered into his ear. "Jim. If you want me to let you come, I will. Do you want to shoot, Jim?"

He nodded and grunted into the gag.

"Really, Jim? Do you really want to shoot your load?"

More vigorous nods and grunts.

"OK. I'll suck you off until you come. God knows you've earned it. I promise you it'll be one of the most intense orgasms of your life." I pulled his cock into my mouth again and sucked him right up to the edge again before breaking off. He groaned again, sounding near to tears in his frustration.

"Only there's a catch," I went on. "If you want to come, you have to do something for me, first. You have to let me replace that plastic cock in your ass with a real one. Mine. You have to let me fuck you, Jim. Let me fuck you, and I'll reward you with the best blow job you've ever had. Otherwise, no orgasm for you. I'll hose you off with cold water and you can go home with blue balls." I paused to let him think it over.

"Do you still want to come, Jim? Don't worry - I'm HIV-negative, but I'll use a condom anyway. There's no chance that you'll catch anything. I know it's a change in the rules we agreed on, so I'm going to take the gag out of your mouth so you can tell me if you agree to the change." I slipped the gag out and asked him again "Do you still want to come?"

His "yes" was a whisper, barely audible over the rasping of his breath.

"What's that, Jim? Say it louder."

"Yes," he said.

"Yes, what? What do you want, Jim?"

"Yes, I want to come. Please let me come."

"You know what the deal is, but I have to hear you say it. What has to happen before I let you come?"

"You're going to... to..."

"Say it, Jim."

"To fuck me." Jim's voice was back down to a whisper.

"Louder, Jim. What do you want me to do?"

"Fuck me." Then a little louder, "Fuck me."

"That's it, Jim. Ask me again," I said.

"Fuck me, Alex."

"LOUDER, YOU ASSHOLE!"

"FUCK ME! PLEASE FUCK ME, ALEX!"

"How do you want me to fuck you, Jim? Come on, beg for it!"

"UP THE ASS! FUCK MY ASS, PLEASE! OH, GOD, PLEASE, FUCK ME UP THE ASS!"

"That's it! Beg for it, pussyboy! Tell me how bad you want my cock!" While he continued shouting out ever-more-colorful descriptions of the act that was about to happen, I pulled five pounds of weight out of his ball bucket, leaving just two inside. Then I moved around behind him and loosened the rope that was holding the dildo inside Jim's ass.

I gently eased the plastic cock out, then slipped a condom on my own. I was so keyed-up for this that I was glad the condom was there, just to cut down on the sensation. Still, even with the extra insulation, Jim's first experience with anal sex was not going to last very long.

I greased up my cock and pressed it up against Jim's hole. It slipped in very easily, thanks to the stretching from the dildo that had just come out. As I sank my shaft into Jim's hot guts, I moaned, completely lost in the sensation.

I forced myself to keep it gentle as I began to pump my cock in and out. I could feel the play of his exhausted muscles against my own as he fought with his dwindling strength to keep himself up on his toes. My fingers fondled and squeezed his nipples, and I gave his cock a few strokes, too - not enough to bring him all the way off, just enough to keep him rock-hard and dripping.

Jim struggled to keep up his recitation as waves of unfamiliar sensation coursed through his body, but his speech made less and less sense as time went on, until he was reduced to a nearly unintelligible "fuck me... fuck me... fuck me...". I was past the point of being gentle. My cock was pounding in and out of him, but fortunately, he wasn't complaining.

I held back and held back as long as I could, but all too quickly, I felt power building up in my groin. Unable to stop the flood, I rammed into Jim for a few final strokes. A huge, guttural moan poured out of my lips as jets of white-hot fire erupted from my cock and filled the balloon stuffed in Jim's ass.

One last thrust, and I withdrew, my cock still achingly hard and twitching as I stripped off the condom. I slipped around to Jim's front side and dropped to my knees. His cock was jumping with each beat of his fast-pounding heart. I enveloped it with my mouth and sucked him for all I could.

My fingers played with his greased-up ass, slipping occasionally inside his still-stretched hole as I sucked. In less than a minute, I could tell he was near, so I slowed down the pace to a crawl. I kept him right on the edge for nearly five minutes, driving him crazy with the desire to come but never quite letting him get there.

Finally, it was time. I increased the speed and pressure, and this time I didn't back off. Seconds later, a great gout of lava shot into my mouth, followed by one, two, three, four, five more in rapid fire. I kept sucking, letting the hot juice overflow out of my mouth to be caught in my waiting hand. With my other hand I took off the ball weights and unsnapped the parachute harness, still sucking all the while.

When at last his moans changed in meaning from "yeah, more" to "stop now!" I let his cock slip from my mouth. I stood up, spat the rest of his load into my hand, and smeared his juices all over his beautiful, sweat-streaked chest. There was enough to coat him from from one gorgeous nipple to the other, from his neck down to his navel. I left it to dry while I worked on the ropes that held him.

First the legs, then the wrists. I released the last one and he slipped down into my arms. I half led, half carried him to the bed where I had first bound him and laid him down on it. I pulled off the blindfold, then unlaced the hood and pulled it off his head. Finally, I unclasped his neck chain and dropped it to the floor. Jim lay curled on his side, so I got down next to him and spooned up against him from behind.

After a long while, Jim opened his eyes and turned to look at me. "I don't know what to say," he said.

"You don't need to say anything, Jim."

We lay in silence for a while longer. Knowing that he was certain to have some ambivalent feelings about what had just happened, though, I got us talking again. He was still straight, I assured him, in case he had any doubts. One ass-reaming experience under duress couldn't change the fact that what made him horny was buxom blondes.

We talked about how well he stood up to the punishing ordeal I had given him, with me heaping lavish praise on his stamina and masculinity. We talked about what, exactly, I had done to him, what he had enjoyed and what he hadn't.

And finally we talked about Michelle.

"I can't believe she didn't mind," he said.

"Why not?"

"It's just not like her. I'm just... surprised. She sounded so completely... bland, you know? Like she was talking about the weather."

"Well, my advice would be to not mention it. Only talk about it if she does."

"But she SAW me, hung up like a... well, like that. I still can't believe she said she was OK with it..."

"Are you sure that's what she did, Jim?" I got up and walked across the room to a darkened corner.

"Sure I'm sure! You heard her, too! She was standing right there..." his voice trailed off as I clicked a button on the computer that was sitting in the corner. My voice came first, followed by Jim's wife's. "'Do you have a minute to take a look at something, Michelle? I want to make sure it's OK with you.' 'Oh, of course it will be, Alex. You know I always like what you guys do here.'"

It had taken me a lot of fiddling around with a sound editor to get everything right - taking out the extraneous noises, adding the appropriate reverberation quality to make it seem like our voices were speaking in an enclosed basement instead of outside by the garden. I'm no professional sound technician, but hey, I "work with computers", right? I can do anything!

Jim sat, speechless, as the whole conversation played through again. Comprehension slowly sank in as he reviewed the last hour of his life. Finally, a smile broke out across his face as he said "You son of a... !"

I grinned back. "Michelle and I were talking about the grape vines and the tomato plants. What did YOU think we were talking about, hmm, you dirty-minded pervert?"

Jim collapsed backward on the bed and laughed. "I can't believe you did that. I can't believe it."

I came back over and sat next to him. The smell of the semen drying on his chest filled my nose. "I told you I was going to mess with your mind, didn't I?"

"So Michelle has no idea, then?" he asked.

"Michelle knows only whatever you've already told her, because

I haven't said a word," I answered. Then, more soberly, "Jim, I know it's early to be thinking about this, but you're going to be leaving soon and I want to throw a thought out to you before you go.

"I had a great time today. I hope you did, too. If you ever want to try this, or something like it, again, you just let me know. I'll be happy to work you over again, although I'll never be able to get your adrenalin flowing the way I did this first time, since you'll have a better idea of what to expect. But I think I can still find ways to keep you entertained.

"I'll also be happy to trade places, and let you get some payback, if that's what you want. And I know Noel would like a chance to get his hands on you, too - he's into three-ways the way I'm into ropes. Although managing the child care issues would take a little more work.

"Or," I continued, "if you want, we can never speak of what happened here again. Personally, I hope that's not what you choose, but the decision is entirely up to you. Don't say anything now - think it over first. Take all the time you want. Noel and I aren't going anywhere, and the offer is always open.

"Now how about you get cleaned up so you can go meet your family? I've got to straighten up down here, too, before Noel and Taylor get home."

We walked upstairs. Jim got dressed in the change of clothes he had brought over and we had a beer in the kitchen, talking about nothing in particular. Then he went back to his place to take a shower, and I headed downstairs to tidy up. I thought as I worked that it was a shame he was going to wash all that beautiful dried cream off his chest.

But I got a nice hard-on thinking about how I might help him do it.

Jim was off at the beach until Sunday night, then he was back to work again on Monday. I had told Noel about our basement encounter, and the open invitation I had left. But even though Jim and I saw each other a few times over the next two weeks, it was always just a brief, slightly self-conscious "hello" as he took out the trash or started out for a run.

Then on Saturday, Noel and I were sitting on the back porch, enjoying the sun while Taylor napped. Jim came out to mow his lawn. He waved hello to us as he fired up his mower.

He was wearing socks and sneakers.

And his tight little red shorts.

And nothing else.

Noel and I exchanged glances, put down our books, and settled back to enjoy the show.

I Want Your Body

This was the thing that Paul always hated about doing the grocery shopping for his wife - what to do when the store didn't have the things on her list.

Ordinarily, Anne Marie did the shopping. Each weekend she would go over the coupons and the sale ads in the paper and write down a detailed list of what to get and how much. Then on Monday she would stop on her way home from work and pick up a week's worth of supplies.

She was very good at finding discounts. They had shopper's club cards at three different grocery stores because Anne Marie knew that Colgate toothpaste, for example, was fifty cents cheaper at PriceChopper than it was at Giant, except when Giant ran its sale every eight weeks, and combining the sale with the doubled coupon meant they could get their toothpaste for half of what they would otherwise pay... and so on for the other several dozen items they typically bought.

Paul had no head for such things himself. If it were up to him, the house would be responsible for all the grocery purchases. What was the point of having a smart refrigerator if you weren't going to listen when it told you you needed to buy more orange juice?

But bargain-hunting made Anne Marie happy, and making his wife happy was the most important thing in the world to Paul. To him, her coupon-clipping habit was a harmless eccentricity - a pointless one, to be sure, but kind of charming, too. Paul pulled in a six-figure salary at the financial services firm where he worked, and Anne Marie earned a respectable amount herself doing graphic design for an advertising agency. Even though the cost of living around San Francisco was astronomically high, they certainly didn't need to be clipping coupons to keep a roof over their heads.

Still, Anne Marie had come from a humble background, and thriftiness was the paramount virtue in her world. Paul was, in fact, secretly proud to watch her plan her weekly assaults on each of the three stores, a one-woman army attacking the bastions of the grocery-industrial complex. It was just one of the many things he loved about her.

But...

Every once in a while, Anne Marie couldn't do the shopping, and so the job fell to Paul. Like this week, when the entire art department at her company was having an over-dinner planning meeting. Paul didn't mind - he loved his wife so much he would move mountains for her; cutting short his evening workout and picking up a cartful of food was trivial. She even made it easy for him - she drew up separate lists for each of the three stores, carefully laid out so that the items on the list were in the order he would encounter them as he worked his way through the aisles.

The one flaw in the plan was what to do when the specific items she listed weren't on the shelves. There were a number of possible solutions to the problem, and he was never sure which was the right one in any given situation.

Sometimes the right answer was to buy something similar. Other times the right answer was to try one of the other stores. Still other times the right answer was to not buy anything at all. It all depended on what the item was.

At this moment, the right answer was not at all obvious.

The list said "McCormick baking powder," but there was no

McCormick baking powder on the shelf. There was a store brand, and there was a brand called "Clammer Round," but no McCormick.

Sometimes Anne Marie insisted on the brand, either because the sale only applied to that brand or because she preferred the flavor. Other times the brand was a preference, not a requirement, so an off-brand would do in a pinch.

Paul tried to think if baking powder was something they needed immediately or if it was just a restock-the-pantry purchase. Was there a birthday coming up that Anne Marie would be baking a cake for? Then maybe the flavor would matter and she had to have the McCormick. Or maybe they were totally out of it and any powder would do. Or maybe it was for deodorizing the refrigerator. Or was that baking soda, not powder? He had no idea. What did one use baking powder for, anyhow?

Calling Anne Marie, his usual fallback, was not an option. Paul tried very hard to be Anne Marie's invincible hero in shining armor. Interrupting her meeting for a question about baking powder was not something that an invincible hero would do.

The entire situation was frustrating, and frustration was not an emotion Paul Mariner was accustomed to. He was not a man to be thwarted or trifled with. He was 27 years old and stood six feet two inches tall. Powerful, well-toned muscles covered his body. A carefully planned regimen of weight, cardio, and martial arts workouts ensured that his body stayed in tip-top shape. And his dominance was not only physical - he was a ruthless shark in the world of commercial real estate deals, netting over $200,000 each year to prove it. Physically and mentally, he was an intimidating presence, and few people ever dared to get in his way.

And yet, here he stood, brought low by a $2.79 can of baking powder.

While Paul dithered, a nasal voice suddenly boomed from directly behind his left ear. "Carl! Carl, how the hell are you!"

With reflexes like a cat, Paul whirled around to find a hand stuck out at him. He grasped it and shook while its owner continued to talk. "How long's it been, huh, gotta be nine, ten years?" The hearty smile began to waver a bit as it became obvious that Paul was not reacting as expected.

Paul carefully disengaged his hand. "Sorry, buddy, but I think you're looking for someone else."

The smile disappeared from the stranger's face. The man was overweight and acne-scarred. He had black, greasy hair and pale, blotchy skin that quivered as he moved his arm back down to his side. His dark eyes were distorted by thick lenses, yet there was something about them that drew Paul's gaze. Paul found himself staring into those black eyes as if they were physically holding his own captive.

"Perhaps," said the stranger in a completely different voice. The forced joviality was gone. His eyes trailed downward, taking the measure of Paul's body from his head down to his toes with a generous pause just below his waist, then back up to meet Paul's gaze once again. "Or perhaps you're just the man I'm looking for."

Paul was disgusted. One of the drawbacks of being handsome and muscular in the Bay Area was the constant attention he got from other men. It was worst at the gym where he worked out - it seemed like every other day some guy tried to hit on him - but there was not a single place he could go where he was guaranteed not to run into some faggot treating him like a piece of beef.

In his younger, brasher days he had thrown a few punches by way of a response, but nowadays he was usually polite - forceful, but polite - when deflecting unwanted advances. Truly, he didn't care what two men might do in private, but he drew the line at when they tried to drag their perversions out into public view. He especially didn't like being the focus of their attention. The thought of some guy fantasizing about Paul's body and imagining the things he would like to do to it made Paul's skin crawl.

A quick image of himself smashing the man's thick glasses and bloodying his nose flashed through Paul's mind. He gained control of himself, though - one of the benefits of aikido training was the mental discipline - and instead said through gritted teeth, "I'm not interested."

The stranger nodded, slowly. Then suddenly he was all smiles again. "My fault, friend, you look just like my old pal Carl from law school. Man, I haven't seen him in ages. Well, sorry to have bothered you. You take care, now," he called over his shoulder as he disappeared from view around the corner of the aisle.

Paul watched the spot where he had vanished for a quarter of a minute, then blinked and turned back to the baking powder, focusing once more on what to do about the missing McCormick's and barely aware of the tingling in his palm where the stranger's hand had touched it.

A little after 9:00 in the evening, Paul was dozing on his bed. He had stripped down to his underwear and was lying on top of the covers. Even though the temperature in the house was cool, sweat sheened his body.

"Hi, sweetie," he heard Anne Marie call from the front door. He tried to return her greeting, but he just couldn't muster the energy. Every muscle in his body felt like it had been pushed past its limit at the gym. Even turning his head was tiring.

He listened to the sounds Anne Marie made as she swept into the house, depositing bags and papers on various flat surfaces as she passed. He heard her putting away the groceries that he had left out on the kitchen counter. The fact that he had left them out would worry her rather than anger her, he knew, because he was usually far too organized to let something like that go. He tried again to muster the energy to call to her, but he just couldn't do it.

At last he heard her on the stairs, calling his name and sounding increasingly unnerved. She slid into the darkened bedroom and was visibly relieved to find him there.

Paul smiled as she came into the room. Even after three years of marriage, he still felt like a newlywed. Anne Marie was a firecracker of a woman, standing only about five-foot-one (without the three-inch heels that she nearly always wore) but carrying herself as if steel beams reinforced her spine. Her dark hair was cut to a medium length and swirled around her head every time she walked.

Her family was originally from Spain, but had spent the last two or three generations in Argentina. Anne Marie's grandfather, Raoul Vilpe, had managed a prosperous business there importing luxury goods. Upon his death, he had left it to his three children - one of them Anne Marie's mother - who managed it with equal success. The first three years of young Anne Marie's life were comfortably wealthy.

Then Argentina went through another of the economic and political convulsions that seemed to grip the country every few decades. Just like in the "dirty war" of the 1970s, the wealthy and powerful became targets of the new government. The Vilpes were accused of making their profits through collusion with corrupt officials of the previous regime. Business slowed, then slowed again. Acts of vandalism at their shop, petty at first, soon grew increasingly frequent and less petty until one night, the building was torched. Worse, Anne Marie's father vanished from a busy street in broad daylight. They never learned what happened to him.

Other family members were facing their own troubles from the new government. The not-exactly-widowed Janita Vilpe de Arrondez and her two young daughters bounced from relative to relative for a while, but the situation grew impossible to stand. No longer willing to depend on the charity of family members, Janita finally fled northward to the United States, using the last of the family savings for plane tickets to Los Angeles.

Once there, she melted into the underground economy and set to work. No job was too menial. She did housekeeping, garment manufacturing, even field labor, her eyes always fixed on her goal of bringing her daughters out of the poverty she had fallen into. She ensured that education was their top priority, and that they were constantly surrounded by reminders of the rewards that come from hard work. She wangled citizenship for her daughters and even Anglicized their names, the better to open the doors of opportunity. Anna Maria Arrondez became Anne Marie Arrons; her sister Catarina became Catherine.

Through their mother's tireless efforts, Anne Marie and Catherine grew up with an aristocrat's sense of self-esteem and a pauper's sense of the value of money. They both attended college, and both got high-paying jobs afterward, Anne Marie in art and Catherine in law.

Once, when both girls were grown and established and making enough money that they could move Janita to a nice condo in a good neighborhood, Anne Marie asked her mother how she could have taken such a gamble. "You had nothing, Mamita. You took a blind chance and it paid off wonderfully, but how did you get the courage to do it?"

"Nothing in life is certain, Anne Marie," Janita replied. "No one can see the future. Sometimes, you find yourself in situations where you cannot possibly know what effect your actions will have. You could spend hours or days or years dithering about what to do, but in the end the result is the same: you just have to act. Do something. Just act."

Her fiery attitude was not the only thing Anne Marie inherited from her mother. The Spanish heritage was evident in her appearance - she had the Conquistador's nose, the flashing black eyes, the proud uplifted chin. Her movements were graceful and precise, every motion of her slender body swift and unerring like a carefully placed shot from an archer's bow. Every time Paul saw her move he felt like he was watching a performance of a tango.

Usually, the mere sight of her walking into a room was enough to move Paul to lift her in his arms and smother her with kisses. This night, a smile was all he could manage.

Anne Marie felt his forehead and was not surprised to find him feverish. Without hesitation, she ran some tepid water in the bathtub and tried to get him into it.

"OK, honey, you need to get in the bathtub, OK, sweetie? You've got a very high fever and we need to get it down. Come on, baby, you can do it," she cajoled. Paul forced himself up, his muscles groaning in protest the whole way. He let her lead him into the tub, where he lay down in the cool water.

"I think I've got the flu or somethin'," Paul said, his voice weak and slurred.

"You just rest, lover, we'll have you better in no time."

Paul spent fifteen minutes in the tub, then crawled back into bed. His wife fussed about him, making sure he was comfortable and that he drank some water and took some Tylenol. As she was about to go back downstairs, Paul said "Honey?"

"Yes, baby?" Anne Marie answered.

"Just in case this is... you know... something serious, there's something I want to tell you."

"Don't talk like that, Paul," she said.

"I just want you to know that... they were out of McCormick baking powder, so I bought Clammer Round instead. I hope that's OK." He was smiling, though it clearly was costing him.

She smiled back, shaking her head. "When you're feeling better, remind me to smack you with a pillow," she said.

Paul spent a fitful night tossing and turning. His muscles were constantly in motion, from tiny twitches in the small muscles of his face to full-force kicks of his legs. His body was like a furnace, radiating so much heat that Anne Marie could feel it from the other side of the bed. More than once she tried to take him to the emergency room, worrying that such a high fever had to be causing him damage. But each time she tried to get him to go, he refused.

"It's just the flu," he told her after her third attempt. "I'm fine."

"Damn machismo," she muttered in reply. "All right, but if you still have this temperature in the morning, I am going to drag you to the doctor and I don't think you'll be able to stop me."

By the time the sun rose, neither of them had gotten more than two hours of sleep. To Anne Marie's obvious relief, Paul's fever was down a bit and the uncontrolled twitching was greatly reduced, though he still felt lethargic and weak. He found himself to be ravenously hungry, which surprised him a bit. He had only been sick a few times in his life, but each time his appetite had been knocked way down, not up.

Not so this time. In half an hour, he plowed through three cheese-drenched eggs, half a pound of bacon, six slices of toast, four glasses of orange juice, and an entire box of wheat chex. Seeing that his appetite at least was healthy, Anne Marie relented on her threat, but only on the condition that Paul take the day off from work to rest. Paul grumbled a bit, but he was too tired to put up much of a fight and agreed. He left a message with the sim-receptionist in his office's comm-net, then stumbled upstairs and finally fell into a deep sleep.

Once it was clear that Paul was sleeping restfully and likely to stay that way, Anne Marie went off to work. She left a note on the bed for Paul to call her the instant he woke up.

Paul woke around noon, feeling completely refreshed. He saw the note, smiled, and told the house to place the call. The wall display turned itself on, showing a generic communication icon instead of video since the call was voice-only.

"Hi, honey," he said when the connection was established.

"Paul, baby, how are you feeling?"

"I'm 100% better, love. Whatever it was, I'm over it."

"Are you sure?" she asked. "You're not just telling me what I want to hear?"

"No lie. The twitching is gone, and I don't have that tired feeling any more. I haven't checked my temperature yet, since your note said to call you first thing or - how did you word it? - you would 'personally emasculate me in a most painful and irreversible fashion'. Which if I may point out would be counterproductive to you as well as me. But it feels like the fever is gone. I'm fine."

"Well, you check it and make sure after we hang up. Oh, thank God. I was so worried. You scared me so much last night."

"I'm sorry," Paul said.

"You don't be sorry. You just stay healthy! Or I'll have to kill you, you know."

"You know that one of the things I love about you is how you never let logic get in your way," Paul said.

"Are you going in to work?" Anne Marie asked.

"I might try," he said. "But believe it or not, I'm hungry again. I think I'm going to roust up some lunch first."

"OK, Paul. You call me if you need anything. And be careful! I love you."

"I love you, too." Paul clicked off the phone.

"Some lunch" turned out to be a four-inch-think, foot-long roast beef sub from Moyo's place on the corner, washed down by a quart of water. Paul was surprised at his food intake. He was a big guy and had been known to pack it in from time to time, but the last time he had put away this much food two meals in a row he had been a teenager. He wasn't worried, though. He was feeling just fine again.

Weeks passed, then months. Paul and Anne Marie spent five days backpacking in Montana, and later another four in Las Vegas. The economy in the Bay Area hit one of its periodic slumps, which meant that there were plenty of forced-to-sell properties available for Paul the shark to snatch up. They went to the wedding of Paul's sister - her second. Neither Paul nor Anne Marie thought it would last any longer than her first, but they smiled and toasted the happy couple all the same.

Some odd things began happening during this time. Nothing bad, just... unusual. One was that Paul began sleepwalking, something he had never been prone to do before. Perhaps once every week or two, he would wake up to find himself in his kitchen putting slices of bread into the toaster, or in the basement racking up a set of billiard balls, or standing in the pitch-black living room sweating and panting as if he had just run a race.

Strangest of all was the time he awoke to see himself juggling a trio of eggs. Paul had never learned how to juggle, and was astonished to find himself effortlessly keeping all three fragile orbs in the air, as if some talented circus performer were magically guiding his arms. Paul watched entranced as his hands performed feats he never dreamed they were capable of. Then, abruptly, the spell was broken. Three eggs, deprived of the expert guidance that kept them aloft, splattered one by one to the floor. Paul marveled at the feat for a moment, then cleaned up the mess and returned to bed.

The next morning he tried to duplicate the feat, using golf balls instead of eggs. He failed utterly, and gave up after only a few tries. Still, he marveled at the memory of the secret show his subconscious mind had somehow performed every time he thought about it.

Then, one bright October day, Anne Marie came home with the news that she had been selected to be the new head of her company's art department. She was delighted, but the feeling was tinged with some regret. She was pleased with the upward momentum of her career, but worried that the extra time she would be spending on management duties would inevitably take away from what she could spend on her creative work. Paul took her out for a celebratory dinner at Chateau Gasquelle, where she shared her mixed feelings with him.

"... I don't want to sound like I'm insulting him, I think Keller was a good director. But sometimes he just seemed to lack people sense, you know? Like the time he wanted to have Sandra do the layout for Hilson's campaign. You remember that one? Sandra's great at the smart-surface detail work - she can make a flat-surface animation look just like a hologram. But asking her to do a whole layout just overwhelms her. Eventually Adam had to take over and bail her out. Keller should have just given it to Adam in the first place."

Paul nodded and signaled for the waiter to refill their wine glasses. It was an oddity of the times that you could only find real humans working as servers in two classes of restaurant: high-end ones like Gasquelle, and hole-in-the-wall dumps. Everything in between used mobile bots with VR projections of sim-personalities.

"You've got great people skills, Anne Marie," he said. "Look, I know you're nervous about the new responsibilities you're getting, but you're going to make a great director. Obviously, Shu-Wan recognized your abilities and is confident you can handle the work or he wouldn't have given you the position. I'm very proud of you, lover." And he genuinely was. Paul was not one to feel threatened by his wife's successes.

"You're sweet," she replied. "No, I know it'll all be fine, and I know I can do it. But I can't help but wonder if it's really what I want. There's so much administrative work. It's going to cut down the amount of time I can spend doing the actual art, and that's what I enjoy most about my job. Or at least, it's what I used to enjoy, but lately it's been getting to be kind of routine, doing the same sort of thing over and over for different clients, you know? Sometimes all the campaigns just blur into each other. So from that sense, maybe the change to management would be a good thing? It's still scary, though."

"Quit fucking moping, you wetback bitch," said Paul.

Dead silence blanketed the table.

Anne Marie sat frozen, her fork halfway to her mouth. Paul stared at her, a look of horror slowly spreading across his face. He fought to speak, but could not seem to spit any words out. Whole seconds passed.

At last Paul found his voice. "Anne Marie, I am so sorry. I swear to you, I meant to say 'would you please pass the bread'. I would never say something like that to you... well, I know I did just say it, but I don't know how. I mean, I didn't mean it, I don't know how those words came out of my mouth, I am so sorry..." He stammered to a halt and looked pleadingly at her stony face.

Anne Marie slowly set down her fork. When at last she spoke, the fury was barely contained in her almost-whispered voice.

"Paul," she said, "I love you dearly. But I will never, ever tolerate anyone speaking to me like that. Ever. Is that clear?"

The rest of the evening passed with a heavy awkwardness hanging over the pair. The other diners around them noticed the tension, but mostly dismissed it as none of their business. Only one man watched them as they left, a fat, jowly man with a pockmarked face, seated at the bar with a computer unrolled in front of him.

Paul's slip of the tongue at the restaurant turned out not to be an isolated incident. The following Monday night, he was listening to Anne Marie as she described her trips to the various grocery stores, bemoaning the fact that none of them carried the brand of skin cream that she liked any more. Completely without him willing it, his mouth said "And there are children starving in India." The comment wasn't as directly insulting as his previous remark but was still not conducive to marital harmony. The strangest part was that he had no idea why he had said it. It wasn't like him at all.

Two days later, as they were watching the evening news together, he stuck his foot out as she was getting up from the sofa. She tripped over his outstretched leg and spilled hot coffee all over herself and the white carpet. Once again, Paul had no idea why he had done it. It was as if his leg had moved of its own volition, like it had a will of its own. Worse, though, was that even though he wanted to apologize, to help her get up and clean up the mess for her, his body was rocking with helpless laughter, and he couldn't stop it.

Anne Marie was furious. "You think that's funny? What the hell is wrong with you, Paul?"

She stormed out of the room, and the moment she was gone, Paul's laughter stopped. By then it was far too late to try to apologize.

The next day, he called her at work from his office to make lewd suggestions over the phone. He was mortified as he heard all manner of obscenities streaming out of his mouth, starting out merely suggestive but quickly descending into raunch, polyamory, and bestiality. He tried to stop talking and to force his fingers to power off the commport, but his muscles refused to respond to him. The torrent of filth continued until at last Anne Marie broke the link and it was as if a faucet had closed, finally shutting off the flow of words. He called back immediately to grovel yet another apology to her, but she refused to speak to him.

That night, when Anne Marie arrived home, she was seething like a volcano. She stormed up to him. He towered over her, but she stabbed her forefinger into his chest, not caring that he massed nearly twice her body weight.

"Whatever your problem is, mister, you'd better fix it fast!" she informed him. "That little stunt you pulled today was unforgivable! I was in the middle of a meeting with three people who used to be my colleagues but who now work for me, and they could hear every single word! I am in the precarious position of trying to gain their respect, and now thanks to you, they look at me like I'm a cheap whore!"

Paul stood like a statue. He yearned to catch her in his arms and beg her forgiveness, but somehow his muscles wouldn't respond. She swept away from him, walking off her anger in a circuit of the room before coming back to continue her tirade. " I don't understand this, Paul. This is not at all like you. You have changed. You used to be sweet and caring, but now you..."

Paul put his finger over her mouth, interrupting her harangue. "Poor baby," he heard himself say. "You're all overwrought. You're so worked up, and for what? Nothing, really. You know what, my little Spanish flower? I know just what you need. All you need... is a good... stiff... dick." He hefted his wife into the air and threw her over his shoulder.

This is what possession by a demon must feel like, Paul thought. He was like a helpless observer in his own body, powerless to control his own actions. He sat back and watched as the demon carried his wife up the stairs like a sack of potatoes, ignoring her cries and the pounding of her fists on his massively muscled back. He watched as the demon threw the woman he would gladly die for onto the bed. He watched as the demon effortlessly tore off her dress and underclothes, batting away her struggles as if she were a child. He watched as the demon opened the fly to his pants, revealing an obscenely hard erection, not an organ of love but an assault weapon. Then, just as he was about to complete his violation of her, the demon vanished, leaving Paul in control of his body again.

Paul tore himself off of Anne Marie and backed away from the bed, so desperate to get away that he banged into the wall behind him and fell to the floor. He stayed there, cowering and clutching at his head, terrified that the demon would return as suddenly as it had gone. By the time he thought to pay attention to Anne Marie again, she had picked herself up and was holding up the remnants of her dress to cover herself.

She stared at him for a long time, breathing hard with her hair streaming out wildly from her head. Then she turned and stalked into the closet. Paul heard her rummaging through her things. He did not move from his crouching position on the floor. At last she emerged, fully dressed and carrying two large bags.

"I don't suppose it will do any good to say this," Paul whispered, "but I'm sorry."

"Sorry," Anne Marie repeated. "You're sorry. Well, what the hell good does that do?"

"It wasn't me," Paul said. "Please believe me. I didn't do it."

"You didn't do it? Well, then, who did? What, do you have an evil twin brother or something? Sorry, baby, but there's nobody here *but* you. But I'll tell you one thing: you won't ever do it again."

She walked to the door of the bedroom, turned, and said "I'll come by tomorrow to pick up the rest of my things. I won't be alone. I think it would be best if you are someplace else when I get here."

With that, she strode down the stairs and out the door.

Paul did a lot of pacing that night, only sleeping a few fitful minutes at a time. He wanted to call her to talk to her, and even started to tell the house to place the call a dozen times. But what would he say? And so each time he canceled the call before the link went through. After what felt like an eternity, he finally fell asleep around six AM, only to be roused back to wakefulness just half an hour later when the alarm clock screeched in his ear. He debated calling in sick, but remembered that he had a meeting with one of his financial backers at nine o'clock. Missing the meeting would jeopardize the deal he was currently working on, and so he reluctantly dragged his weary body up and into the shower.

Two hours later, he was in his Jaguar on his way to the office. The car was his pride and joy. It was only a year old, and he loved it even though it was rapidly becoming completely impractical. Jaguar was the last remaining holdout among major car manufacturers to resist adding the automation that now came standard with every other car sold. It was an image thing - they marketed their high-end cars to the sort of men who liked to be in control of their vehicles, rather than the other way around.

Thus it couldn't connect to the area's freeway grid. The automatic grid had worked miracles for the region's traffic problems, as it had for major urban centers across the country. It had started out as an experiment that covered only a few restricted-access lanes on the most congested freeways, but the experiment had been such a success that it had been rapidly expanding ever since. There were more cars than ever on the roads, and yet both traffic jams and accident statistics were way down because one central intelligence was driving them instead of a hundred thousand fallible, slow-reacting human brains.

During the morning and evening rush hours, Paul's car was relegated to the "dumb" lanes, those few remaining stretches of asphalt designated for cars that couldn't connect to the grid. Each morning and afternoon, Paul watched the cars in the smart lanes zipping past him at eighty miles an hour, their drivers sipping cups of coffee or doing crosswords or applying makeup or even napping while the regional traffic AI navigated them efficiently to their destinations.

Paul's was usually the only car in the dumb lanes that was less than a decade old, and on a good day there was enough empty space for him to hit sixty MPH. Even though "dumb" cars were steadily being replaced by smart ones, the traffic situation in the dumb lanes never seemed to get any better, but that was because the grid was constantly expanding. Every year, there were fewer and fewer dumb lanes available, and Paul could see the day coming when he wouldn't be allowed on the freeways at all.

Still, he loved his car, and he loved driving it. He also loved the fact that no one else could - it was one of the few manual transmission vehicles still operating in all of California.

Later, sitting in his office, Paul hoped that the bags under his eyes didn't look as bad as they felt. Image counted for a lot in his line of work. It undercut his effectiveness if he showed even a hint of being off his peak. Anne Marie would have been able to help, he thought wistfully. She would have had some kind of makeup or something that he could have used undetectably to cover up the blotches and make him look like he hadn't spent the night on a bender. He desperately hoped that his actions of the night before had not irrevocably destroyed his marriage, that he could somehow win Anne Marie back.

First, however, he would have to ensure that the demon never, ever came back. And he had no idea how to even begin.

Calvin Saunders arrived promptly at nine, and Paul ushered him into the conference room. The point of the meeting was to convince Mr. Saunders to invest in commercial and office space in what used to be a very nasty neighborhood in San Jose. After some initial banter and coffee, Paul slipped into his familiar patter, growing increasingly comfortable as the routine proceeded.

"... the Richmont area is starting to shed its blighted image," he said. "You know, of course, that five, ten years ago it was all housing projects and burned-out storefronts. I wouldn't have recommended that you invest five bucks there, never mind fifty million. But things are changing. The gays are moving in. You know how it goes, they buy a house here, a house there, and soon they're fixing them up, they put up tidy little gardens and white picket fences and smart-fabric curtains with tasteful, subdued animations on them. The graffiti goes down, the property values go up, and suddenly you've got yourself a nice neighborhood again.

"And that's what's happening in Richmont. Gay couples who can't afford San Francisco are discovering San Jose. They don't have kids, so they spend their money on their homes and themselves. It's a perfect place to raze some public housing and put up a lifestyle center. You can't go wrong with this one, Mr. Saunders." Calvin Saunders was one of the few people Paul didn't address by his first name; Mr. Saunders was of a generation that grew up in a more formal world, and made his preferred form of address known to those who dared to presume more familiarity.

Calvin was not impressed by Paul's reasoning. Another

characteristic of his generation, one that he shared with Paul despite the difference in their ages, was a distaste for the increasingly public role homosexuals had begun assuming since even before the turn of the millennium. He was deeply, innately disgusted at the idea of two men pawing at each other. It was perversion, pure and simple.

And so he argued with Paul. "Why the hell should I be subsidizing their lifestyle? That's all it would be. My money to help them do the things they do. No way, Paul. Forget it."

Eventually, however, Paul wore down his resistance. "I couldn't agree with you more," he said, "what they do is immoral. It's disgusting and it's just downright sick. But Mr. Saunders - and please forgive me if I seem out of line here - I think you're looking at it all backward. Don't think of it as *them* using *your* money to do their thing. They don't need your money for that - they've *got* money. What you're doing is using your money to *take theirs away*.

"Think about it," he continued. "All these faggots are going to spend their money somewhere. Why not have them spend it at stores in a building *you own*? Then you can take the profits you make from them and use it to help counter the homosexual agenda. Make donations to churches and decent universities, support family-minded political candidates. There's also some research going on that you might want to fund. A group of scientists claims they're very close to isolating the cause of the disorder, and they're hopeful they can one day cure it right in the womb. Wouldn't that be a fitting use for their money?

"Or you can just keep it. Then, it's not *you* funding *their* lifestyle - *they're* funding *yours*! It's poetic justice, really."

They talked for another half an hour, but Paul had made his point. The rest was just quibbling about details. Eventually, business talk gave way to idle banter, and before too long Calvin had started into a rambling story about his great-granddaughter and her new puppy. Paul gritted his teeth and allowed his mind to wander a bit. This was one part of his job that he wasn't fond of, but it was necessary. He sat listening with half an ear and making appropriate noises at the right places. Idly, he picked up his pen and began toying with it, twiddling it in his fingers while he feigned interest in Calvin's blather. He was pondering the sight of the fog condensing on the conference room window when he happened to look down and saw a sight that froze his heart mid-beat.

There, on his pad, written in capital letters with his own pen by his own hand, were the words "YOU'RE FUCKED, PAUL".

It took only an instant for the meaning of the words to register. When they did, Paul tried to get up from his chair and bolt from the room, but before he could move, the demon had seized control of him again. Once more, he was a captive in his own body, unable to exercise any control while an invisible puppet master pulled his strings.

Paul got up out of his chair, cutting off Mr. Saunders' story with an abrupt interruption. "Let me tell you something, Cal old pal," he said. "I've been thinking here while I've been listening to you, and I've reached a conclusion. I think it's time for us to seriously reevaluate our working relationship.

"You see, Cal," Paul said as he paced back and forth, "my time is a very valuable thing. Up until now, I've been perfectly willing to listen to your endless digressions because you have a lot of money that I want to get my share of. But I just now decided that that is no longer the case. I have been sitting here for ten minutes listening to you drone *on and on* about your sniveling little whelp and her pathetic canine sidekick. Ten minutes is a long time, Cal. There are a lot of ways I would like to spend ten minutes, and not one of them involves listening to your inane rambling."

He walked around the table and crouched down next to the speechless Calvin Saunders. "While I was waiting for you to finish your blithering, I did a little cost-benefit analysis, Cal. I estimated how much it would cost me to not have your fifty million behind my little project versus how much personal, emotional benefit I would reap by kicking your very wealthy but oh-so-tedious ass out the door. And you know what, Cal? This is definitely worth fifty mil."

Paul picked the older man up bodily out of his chair and hoisted him up into a fireman's carry over his broad shoulder. Mr. Saunders sputtered and yowled, but he was helpless against Paul's massive muscles. Paul hauled him through the office's lobby and stabbed the elevator button. The commotion attracted the attention of the rest of the people on the floor. They all stared slack-jawed as the doors opened and Paul dumped Mr. Saunders unceremoniously onto the elevator floor. He reached in and punched the button for the ground floor.

"Good-bye, Cal," he said, "You know what? For fifty mil, that was a bargain."

The doors closed.

Paul turned around and strode back to his office. He grabbed his coat from the hook, put it on and headed back out. On his way through the reception area, the head of the firm stepped into his path and said "Paul, I'd like to see you in my office, please. Right now."

"Sorry, Roddy," said Paul without breaking his stride. "No time right now. How about... never? Does never work for you?"

"Paul, this is unacceptable behav..."

Paul spun, grabbed his boss by the front of his shirt with both fists and pressed him up against the nearest wall. "Mr. Roderick Jackoff-son. Would you kindly shut. the. fuck. up." He released him and continued on to the stairs. No one tried to stop him, and soon he was down twelve flights and out the back door onto the alley behind the building.

The moment the door closed behind him, the demon vanished again. Paul crashed heavily to the ground. A car flashed past on the nearby main street, and he caught a glimpse of Calvin Saunders' large white eyes as his driver accelerated away.

Paul spent the next few hours in a helpless daze. He had no idea how to deal with the changes that had happened during the last sixteen hours. He rambled over to a nearby park where walked and sat while he tried to figure out what was going on.

Was he going insane? He didn't think so. He felt like he was in complete control of his mind. It was his body that he didn't have any control over. As bizarre as it sounded, the only explanation that made any sense was that someone - or something - was somehow controlling him.

But how could that happen? There was no logical way to explain how something could just take over his body whenever it felt the whim. Paul tried and discarded several possibilities before succumbing to the inevitable conclusion he did not want to accept: he was possessed by a demon.

He laughed a short hysterical bark at the thought. Here he was, sitting in a park in twenty-first century America, having thoughts that belonged with the superstitious nonsense of fourteenth-century Europe.

But nothing else made sense. How else could he explain the terrifying sense of being a passenger in his own body while something made him do terrible, inexplicable things?

After a long bout of further thought, Paul allowed himself to provisionally consider the idea, ludicrous as it was. After all, he had to do *something* to get his life back. Surely it was better to take any action at all than to do nothing, even if that action was based on a completely implausible diagnosis of his problem.

So. Where did that leave him? If, hypothetically speaking, he was possessed, then... what was he going to do about it? How do you get help for demonic possession? Paul wasn't a religious man. Was it the Catholics who did exorcisms? Was he insane for even considering such a thing? Would they laugh him out of their church?

After another long bout of staring at nothing, he decided to return to his car, get in, and just drive. He would stop at a church or a psychiatrist, whichever he came to first, and beg for help.

It didn't work out. He came to a Catholic church first. He parked his car and went into the rectory. The priest was there, but when Paul tried to speak, the demon took over and all his words came out garbled, like a recording played backwards. After a frustrating five minutes of trying to be understood, he gave up and fled back to his car.

The psychiatrist that he found was no more help. Paul was able to wheedle his way past the receptionist and actually speak to the doctor. But the demon took over again as soon as the doctor came into the room and kept the conversation at the level of light banter.

"Why exactly are you here, Mr. Mariner?" the puzzled psychiatrist asked after ten minutes of talk about nothing.

"I wanted to speak with you, Dr. Silverine," said the demon.

"About what?"

"Nothing in particular. I've been feeling a little down lately, but it's nothing serious."

"Down in what way?"

"Oh, this and that, I guess. Maybe it's existential angst."

This went on for a long while. Psychiatrists tend to be a patient lot, but even they have their limits.

"I'm afraid I still don't understand, Mr. Mariner," Dr. Silverine eventually said. "You seem like a well-adjusted individual to me. If there is something you would like my help with, you'll have to tell me what it is. Otherwise, how can I help?"

"I don't know, doctor. Perhaps I don't really need help after all. In fact, I'm sure I don't. Although I sincerely appreciate you taking the time to talk with me. Thank you so much," the demon said calmly. Paul's face showed complete serenity even though inside, he was screaming and screaming. The demon lifted his body smoothly out of the chair, made it give the doctor a firm handshake, uttered some banal pleasantries, and walked him back outside to his car.

Then the real nightmare began.

When Paul was a boy, he had nearly drowned once in a drainage culvert. Heavy water after a winter storm had filled the usually dry bed with a rushing torrent. Paul and two friends had been tossing sticks and other debris into the water and watching them swirl and bob in the racing water. With no warning, Paul's foot slipped on a slick patch of ground and he fell into the ditch.

He was a good swimmer, but he was no match for the water's power. He was swept rapidly downstream until the culvert passed under a road. A grate of bars blocked the way, and Paul was pressed up against it. His head was above the surface, but just barely, so water was constantly splashing and spurting into his nose and mouth.

For the next twenty minutes he was trapped, held immobile by the force of the stream. Every breath was a struggle, both against the cold pressure on his chest and against the water soaking his face. His friends raced off for help, and when the paramedics came, they were able to extract him and lift him to safety. Those twenty minutes while he waited, utterly powerless to do anything to help himself, were the most terrifying of his life.

Until now.

One moment, he was sitting behind the wheel of his Jaguar, starting the engine and getting ready to pull away. The next, he was blind and deaf. It was like someone had flipped a switch, cutting Paul off from all light and sound in the blink of an eye.

But his body continued to drive.

He could feel his arms turning the wheel and his legs pushing the pedals. He could feel the G-forces as the car accelerated and rounded curves. But he could not see or hear a thing. It seemed impossible that he would not crash into something.

And yet he didn't. Obviously he wasn't running into things or leaving chaos in his wake, because the Jaguar continued to glide smoothly along. He could feel the car stopping at what had to be traffic lights, accelerating smoothly when the invisible light turned green, eventually merging onto a freeway. When it became clear that the demon was not going to send him to a grisly death - yet, at least - he began to relax, just a bit. He had time to wonder how long his blindness and deafness might last, indeed whether it might be permanent. Then these thoughts led him to speculate about the bigger picture of what the demon might want from him.

His imaginings, horrible though they were, did not come close to what it turned out the demon had in mind. He felt the Jaguar stop and his hand pull the key from the ignition. He got out of the car and walked up to a door. His walk was confident, not fumbling, Paul noted. Obviously his eyes must still be working; something must be blocking their signals from reaching his brain. He pulled open the door and descended some steps into a warm room that stank of liquor, sweat, and cigar smoke. Then, all at once, vision and sound returned to his world.

He was in a large, dimly-lit bar. It could easily have held a hundred or more people, but because of the early evening hour, only about a dozen were there. They were all men, Paul realized, and they were all dressed - in some cases, only partly dressed - in black leather, with gleaming metal adornments. He saw that the walls were covered in pornographic images, pictures of men in cuffs or chains or straps, sucking on each others' cocks or flogging each others' backs. The skin on Paul's neck began to crawl as realized exactly what kind of bar this was.

Still fully under the demon's control, Paul walked up to the bar, slapped his keys down on it, and said "I've got a year-old Jaguar XV-350 sitting outside. It belongs to whichever one of you limp-wristed fairies can make me come without touching my dick."

The leather-clad men looked at one another, then at least half of them got up off the barstools and out of the booths and converged on Paul. One of them grabbed at Paul's sleeve and made to pull him toward a back room. Paul yanked his arm free and said "Only there's a catch. I'm not going to go willingly. You're going to have to fight me."

With that, the demon vanished, and Paul once again had full control over his body. It only took an instant for him to see his chance and he seized it, making a sudden dash for the door. He was halfway there when one of the leathermen tossed a chair into his path. He caught his foot between the legs of the chair and went down. They were on top of him a moment later.

As the demon had promised them, he fought. Reflexes from all his martial arts training kicked in, and he was soon landing solid kicks and punches on his attackers. He bloodied the nose of one of the leathermen with a slam from the heel of his hand, and felt the jaw of another dislocate when his foot struck it.

But there were too many of them. The pack quickly overwhelmed him and in less than two minutes, Paul was lying on the floor with his arms twisted up behind his back and a man sitting on each of his legs. The guy whose jaw he had broken put his foot on Paul's neck and said "I get first crack."

They put cuffs on his wrists and shackled his ankles together with a short length of chain between them. Then they forced him up to his feet. One of the men held him from behind with his immense arm around Paul's neck. The rock-hard muscles squeezed against the veins in Paul's neck. The implied threat was clear: the blood supply to Paul's brain could be completely cut off with a simple flex of a biceps. Paul stumbled forward in chain-shortened steps through a dark hallway and into what could only be described as a dungeon.

He began to plead with his captors, begging them to let him go and saying it was all a mistake. They bought none of it, of course, assuming it was all part of the scene Paul wanted to play. The broken-jawed guy came up right into Paul's face.

"Look, you worthless worm," he said, holding his mouth with one hand. "At this point I don't even care about the car. After what you did to me, all I want is to see you suffer."

They stood Paul in the center of the room and hooked leather cuffs to his wrists. These cuffs were then linked to a pair of chains. The men released the metal cuffs that held his hands together, then winched the chains up until Paul was standing on his toes with his arms spread out wide above his head.

They took his clothing off, slicing roughly through the silk of his suit and tearing open his shirt rather than wasting time undoing buttons. When they had finished, the shredded remains of Paul's clothes lay in a tangled pile in the corner and Paul stood exposed in all his naked glory. His body was extremely impressive, muscled like a Greek god's and coated on his chest, arms, and legs with pale blond fuzz. His cock was a steel flagpole, jutting out from his abdomen and piercing the air. The sight prompted raucous comments from the observers. They whistled and made catcalls and slapped the chained-up hunk's flesh.

Then they began the torture.

Paul's back and ass were paddled and whipped until they felt like they were on fire. Clamps with viciously sharp teeth were attached to his nipples, and weights were hung from them to dangle and cause further pain with every movement of his body. A rough rope was wrapped around his balls, after some mocking discussion about whether that violated the "don't-touch-my-dick" terms of the scene. More weights were hung from the rope, stretching Paul's nuts low in their sac. Paul was hooded and gagged, punched and pinched and slapped. A taser was applied to his waist and thighs, making him dance and writhe in his chains. Through it all, his cock stayed rock-hard and dripping with clear juice.

At last they took him down from the chains. Paul half-hoped that his ordeal was over, but knew deep down that he could not possibly have such luck. Sure enough, the leathermen bent him down over a padded horse, lengthwise, so that his body rested on the surface. They spread his legs wide apart and chained them in place. A collar was locked around his neck and chained to the horse so that he couldn't lift his head. They removed the hood and gag, but quickly replaced the gag with a larger, thicker one that completely filled his mouth and locked behind his head. They left his hands free, but with the locked chains and the position he was in, he couldn't do anything but flap them around uselessly.

Paul waited for the next round of torment to begin, but his pain-fogged mind did not anticipate what it would be until he felt hands slathering grease around his exposed asshole. When it dawned on him what was about to happen, the panicked. He exploded in a frenzy of effort, struggling to break free of the bonds that held him and grunting frantically into the gag that filled his mouth. Nothing helped.

When he felt the tip of a penis poking at his tightly-clenched ass, he redoubled his fruitless efforts. As the invader strove to force itself in past his sphincter, his muffled screams began to rise in pitch. And when at last it succeeded and buried itself deep in Paul's guts, his struggles stopped because all he could focus on was the pain. He could not believe how badly his ass hurt. His sphincter muscles had gone into spasm, and the pain was incapacitating.

At first, the cock just sat there, stuffing his ass but not moving at all. Then, in slow motion like the start of an avalanche, it began to slowly slide in and out. The sensation of friction was added to the feeling of fullness and Paul's breath exploded out through his nose. He had not even been aware he was holding it.

The fucking felt like it went on forever. His rapist was skilled, and made the experience last a good long time. His cock thrust in and out of Paul's ass, grinding against the tender tissues of his rectum and tearing at the sensitive membrane. Occasionally its owner pulled it out completely, only to slam it once more into the trapped and waiting hole. Paul was in agony at first, but as the muscles of his ass steadily stretched, the pain lessened a bit. It still hurt, but not blindingly like before. He heard himself grunting in a deep, growling voice with each of his rapist's thrusts.

After a long while, the pace accelerated, and soon the man behind him was grunting too. Paul couldn't feel it happening, but he could picture the man's cock shooting a load of thick, white semen into his gut. The thought disgusted him so thoroughly that he nearly vomited. With an effort of will, he choked back the bile, knowing that the gag would only trap the mess in his mouth.

When he was spent, the leatherman pulled out with a slushy popping sound. Paul felt a warm trickle dripping down his leg and had to choke down another surge from his stomach, his hands clenching spasmodically in the air.

Then the next man took his turn.

Paul nearly despaired at the thought of having to endure a dozen violations when surviving just one was so hard to do. Mercifully, though, as the third cock was taking its turn pounding in and out of his bleeding hole, he felt his own cock begin to twitch and a familiar churning in his balls. Though he would never have imagined it possible, the sensations were undeniable. He lingered on the edge for an eternity, then convulsed in the throes of a powerful orgasm. His cock was pressed up against the padding of the horse, so his juices dripped down to splat against the bare concrete floor. Paul howled into the gag for what felt like hours.

The clenching of Paul's ass drove the man fucking him to his own climax, and for a short while, the two of them grunted and groaned together. When at last it was over, he pulled out and wiped himself off. Then he smacked Paul's dangling balls with the flat of his hand, causing Paul to jump and yank at his chains.

"The next time you show your face in here," the main said, "try not to be such a shithead."

He walked toward the door. "Come on, Max," he called to the man with the broken jaw, "let's go for a ride in my new car. I'll take you to get your jaw looked at." Most of the men began to trickle out of the room, although two stayed behind to buckle a third into a sling, and a fourth released the locks that held Paul in place.

Paul pulled himself to his feet and gently worked the gag out of his mouth. He stretched his sore jaw.

"I'm Adam," said the man who had unlocked the chains. The room was empty now except for the trio at the sling, now completely absorbed in a suck-and-fuck session.

"Paul." The word came croaking out of his mouth. From the parking lot came the sound of the Jaguar's engine revving up, followed by the crunching sound of the transmission's gears crashing together under the inexperienced hands of its new owner. Paul winced.

"Pardon me if I'm probing where I'm not welcome, " Adam said, "but despite what you said in the bar and the... well, obvious evidence on the floor, I got the distinct impression that you were not enjoying yourself. Am I wrong?"

Paul started to say "No, you're not wrong at all," but the words that came out were "No, that was exactly what I was looking for." Adam looked at him quizzically, but nodded in acceptance.

The demon was in full control again. Paul wanted to beat and destroy something in his anger, fear, and frustration. Instead, the demon calmly accepted Adam's offer of help. Paul walked gingerly to the bathroom to clean up while Adam gathered up the shreds of his clothing. Nothing was usable except the belt, the socks, and the shoes.

"I've got a change of clothes in the car. They'll be a little tight on you, but you're welcome to them," he said. The demon nodded.

Some minutes later, dressed in a nondescript T-shirt and pants, Paul and Adam walked out through the bar. The hazy sky was starting to grow dim as the hidden sun moved lower. "You don't have a car," Adam pointed out. "Can I give you a ride somewhere?"

The demon accepted the offer and sat in the passenger seat. He directed Adam on a ten-minute trip through cramped back streets, stopping him at a nondescript intersection and getting out of the car.

"Are you sure you're all right?" Adam asked.

"It's all good," said the demon. "Really. Thanks for the ride, and the clothes." He stood on the side of the road until Adam slowly drove away.

The demon walked Paul a short way up the street. Both sides were lined with row homes, and Paul couldn't see anything significant about the one that the demon walked into that would distinguish it from all the rest. The door opened easily and the demon shut it behind him. He walked through a short hallway and into a room that had probably once been a parlor when the house was first built. Now it was crowded with a variety of electronic gear.

Seated in one corner of the room, surrounded by screens, keyboards, and wires, was a flabby man with thinning hair and acne scars on his face. He was grinning a nasty, toothy grin.

"Hello, Paul," the man said.

Paul stumbled with the sudden effort of having to hold himself up as the demon departed again. Paul looked back toward the door. "I wouldn't advise it," the man said.

Paul turned back to face him. "Do I know you?" he asked.

"We've never formally met," the man said, "although I've had my eye on you for quite a while now. My name is Fillmore. We've shaken hands once, but it wouldn't surprise me if you didn't remember me. Most people don't find my face a particularly memorable one. Why don't you have a seat and I'll tell you about our previous encounters."

Paul hesitated, but eventually cleared a pile of papers, discs, and cubes off of a chair and sat down in it. As drained as he was from his recent ordeal, it was still clear to Paul that this Fillmore very likely had some explanation for the hell that his life had become in the last twenty-four hours. Part of him wanted to release a day of pent-up tension and beat the answers out of him until he was a bloody pulp. Another part recognized that any such attempt would almost certainly be blocked by the demon. He decided to wait.

"I'm sure you want an explanation of what's been happening to you," Fillmore said. "And I have one for you. Which I'll get to in a bit. First, I want to tell you a little bit about me.

"As you can see, I'm fat, I'm ugly, and I'm... no, no, it's true. Don't try to spare my feelings and tell me otherwise. I'm also very smart, but that doesn't tend to attract women. Or men. Which is where my interests lie."

Despite himself, Paul couldn't stop his face from giving away his reaction to this news. He got his expression back under control quickly, but it was obvious Fillmore had seen.

"I know that you're not very fond of homosexuals, even before your happy little gang-bang at the bar just now. You usually put on a good show of hiding it, showing everyone how sophisticated and tolerant you are. But deep down, you find the idea of two men getting it on repugnant. Hey, to each his own opinion. You're entitled to think whatever you want."

"How do you know about the bar? In fact, how do you know so much about me in the first place?" Paul interjected.

"I'll get to that. Just bear with me a little longer. My problem has always been one of trying to attract partners. Physical attractiveness is very highly prized in the gay world. I haven't got it. No one wants to be with a fleshy blob like me. I tried doing something about it, but I found I just didn't have the willpower for the whole eat-right-and-exercise thing. I like food; I hate sweating. I spent four months once being constantly hungry, sore, smelly, and exhausted, and all I had to show for it was a paltry ten pounds and my face was still a mess. It just wasn't worth it.

"One day it dawned on me that I was working too hard at something I was inherently not good at. I should instead be focusing on my strengths instead of my weaknesses. And I happen to be very, very smart, and very, very good at software.

"I don't know if you're aware of this, but nobody actually writes software any more, not in the old meaning of the term. These days systems are so complex that they can only be created by other systems. The role of the human is to guide the creation process. That's what I do. Are you familiar with nano-technology,

Paul?"

"Sure," Paul answered. "Tiny machines, smaller than a cell. They're used a lot in medicine, fighting tumors, stuff like that."

"Right. Everyone knows about the medical applications because that's what finally ended AIDS. But nanotech is everywhere - in communications, in media, agriculture, and a host of other places. Individually, each nano-machine is about as smart as a goldfish... no, not even that smart. A flatworm, maybe. Just a bundle of limited stimulus-response behaviors. But even a small space can hold billions of them, and when they all work together, they can create a system that is very smart indeed.

"To solve my problem, I created a system and introduced it into my body. It was supposed to assist me in getting myself into better shape. It worked, even, to a degree. The machines lined themselves up along my nerve pathways, creating in effect a second parallel nervous system. They stimulated my muscles while I slept, causing the fibers to contract without me having to force myself through the effort of lifting weights or running. Other machines slowed my digestion, so more calories passed through me unabsorbed. They even cleaned up my acne.

"And you know what? In two months, I lost five more pounds, and I was just as hungry, sore, and exhausted as ever. And my face hurt all over. I could tell the net to suppress the pain, but that would have been pointless. The problem that I finally had to face was that I was trying to be somebody I wasn't. My body wants to look like this, no matter how much my mind may wish otherwise. And no nanosystem would ever be able to help."

Paul said "I'm sorry to hear that, but what does that have to do with...?"

"With you?" Fillmore interrupted. "Well, it was clear that my body would never be a lean, powerful muscle machine. If I wanted to have the perfect body, I would have to find another way to get it. Once I framed the question that way, the solution became obvious. I would just find a body that was already perfect and use that one."

The hairs began to stand up on the back of Paul's neck.

"So I started working on my next system. Do you remember some months ago, you were standing in the grocery aisle staring at the shelves? I came up to you and shook your hand. You thought I was hitting on you. But during that handshake, I transferred some nanomachines from my palm to yours. They immediately began to reproduce and infect you. You probably felt very ill and feverish that night, and hungry afterward. Yes? You do remember, it seems."

"You son of a bitch!" Paul shouted, leaping to his feet. Papers and electronics crashed messily to the floor. The urge to start pounding on this arrogant bastard was overwhelming. "You infected me? You put little machines in my blood?" he said, advancing on the place where Fillmore sat. "Well, you are going to get them all back out again, you filthy little..."

Paul's voice cut off abruptly and he froze in mid-stride. Deprived of all muscle control, he tipped slowly over and crashed heavily to the cluttered floor.

"Paul," Fillmore said, "I know this is hard for you to accept, but there is absolutely nothing you can do. Now be a good boy and sit." The demon took over then. It got Paul up off the ground, walked him meekly back to the chair, and sat him down. Paul raged impotently.

Fillmore went on. "The way the system works is this: you now have a network just like mine. It runs parallel to your nervous system. Every sensation you receive through your nerves, the net also receives. Every impulse you send out to your muscles, the net monitors. But it's not just passive - the net can intercept the signals coming in from your body and make sure they never reach your brain. Likewise, they can trap the impulses leaving your brain and ensure they never reach your muscles. They can also generate substitute signals in either direction.

"You've seen the results. I can turn your eyes and ears, all your senses in fact, on and off at will. I can make you dance, juggle, sing opera... whatever I want you to do."

"But this is impossible," said Paul, finding himself able to move his head but not the rest of his body. "No technology on Earth is advanced enough to do what you claim."

"Do you want to dispute the evidence of your own eyes?" Fillmore snapped. "It's real, all right. Here, do you want another sample? Do you remember how you felt when you were blind and deaf? Well, I am about to turn off *all* your senses. Not just sight and hearing, but taste, touch, smell, proprioception, everything. Here goes."

Paul was instantly gone. There was no other way to describe it. He no longer had a body. There was no light, no sound, no air, no gravity. All the tiny background processes of life were gone - his breathing, his heartbeat, the flow of saliva in his mouth, the steady rumble of his digestion. All gone.

He was lost in nothingness. His entire universe was a void. The absence of external stimuli was not too bad, no worse than being in a dark quiet room. If he had to endure such sensory deprivation for a long time, then it would no doubt begin to bother him, but not yet.

No, the real terror came from his missing body. The absence of any feedback from the physical structure that was his mind's only home was terrifying. He yearned to feel anything at all, to twitch his finger or swallow or blink, but there was nothing. Nothing at all. He had no body.

Panic set in.

Then, abruptly, he was back. Despite the panic of his mind, his body was relaxed and calm. No adrenalin sang in his blood and his breathing was smooth and even. The mismatch between his mind and his body was jarring, making Paul feel like he was a stranger in his own skin.

"That was one minute," Fillmore said. "Would you like to try an hour?"

Paul shook his head.

"And that was nothing compared to what I can do. That was just turning off a switch. No artistry in it at all. I told you, I'm very, very good at what I do, and I'm looking forward to working through all of the possibilities that our new symbiosis allows. Although I must say, you were almost right. No technology on Earth is capable of this... except mine."

"But even if that's true," Paul said. "How can your net possibly exercise such control? Even if you can make my muscles contract whenever you want, how can you make me coordinated enough to juggle?"

"Oh, I don't control you at the level of individual nerve fibers," replied Fillmore. "I deal in whole systems. You do the same thing - you don't tell your individual muscles to flex one at a time. You think in high-level terms like 'catch a baseball' or 'shift to third gear' or 'kiss my wife'. My machines spent several months just observing you, learning how you work and compiling a dictionary of high-level commands. Every move you made was recorded, analyzed, and converted into an entry in my dictionary. You'd be surprised how simple it is, really. You only have a few hundred basic movements in your vocabulary. They combine together in various ways to make a huge variety of possibilities, but at its core, your whole repertoire fits into a very small table in a data store. Likewise with your senses.

"When I want you to do something, I just tell your system to activate the right combination of movements. I can do it by voice. Watch this: Simon says, 'clench your right fist'."

Obediently, Paul's right hand clenched into a fist. He tried, knowing it was futile, to open it up, and was unsurprised to fail.

"Simon says 'do jumping jacks'."

Paul obeyed. As he bounced up and down, Fillmore continued talking. "Did you catch what the system did there? In order to carry out the command, it knew it first had to stand up. I didn't have to specify that, it figured it out on its own. OK, Simon says 'sit down'."

Paul did. Fillmore took him through several more postures and movements, leaving Paul feeling steadily more hopeless with every stunt his body performed.

Then, "Simon says 'get an erection'."

To Paul's shame and horror, he did. His penis swelled, steadily tenting the front of his pants.

Fillmore said "Have an orgasm."

Paul waited for the inevitable, but strangely, nothing happened. After a few moments, he looked over at Fillmore, who grinned nastily, shook his finger and said "Ah, ah, ah, I didn't say 'Simon says'."

The nasty smile faded. "But voice control is so primitive. I much prefer using a direct link between my net and yours."

He told Paul how the two nets were capable of communicating. They translated sensory input and motor output into a common symbolic representation, which could then be used to translate sensations and motions between the networks. If he chose to do so, Fillmore could see, hear, and feel everything that Paul did. And, operating in reverse, he could make Paul's muscles act out any impulse that originated in Fillmore's brain.

"Of course," he said, "I suppress my own motor responses while I'm controlling you. I don't want to be walking into walls or anything.

"The two networks can communicate with each other directly without significant signal degradation over about a 200-meter range, using only the power from our own cellular processes for energy. Much further apart than that and the signal begins to get noisy. I can still control you remotely from as far away as a kilometer if there are no obstructions, but there's a noticeable time lag and it's a very disorienting experience.

"For times when you're farther away from me, I still have some options. One is to install repeaters to boost the signal in certain selected locations. I did that near your home and in your car and also at... well, I'll get to that later. When I need more mobility I can have you carry a battery-powered transceiver. And then another possibility is to send commands in batch mode, packets of instructions that are stored and then executed later. The net is capable of some limited autonomy, so that if you're walking, for instance, over a rough surface, it's smart enough to be able to keep you upright and moving. Or if you encounter a hole, it knows to either stop or jump across. But if you come across someone you know, it's not smart enough to make you stop and say hello. That needs my intervention."

Paul's sense of despondency deepened as Fillmore continued to talk. After a time, Fillmore began to digress into the technical details of how the system worked, and Paul got lost in jargon that he didn't understand. Eventually he gave up even trying to listen, lost in his private despair.

After a particularly long stretch of techno-babble, there finally came a pause. Paul looked up and said "Why me?"

"Why you?" Fillmore echoed. "Well, it's not much of a reason, but the truth is it's because I like the way you look. Nothing more. I just went to a gym one day and picked you out. I slipped a locator onto you, found out where you lived, who you were, what your routine was. I got a DNA sample from some of your hair and keyed my nanomachines to it. Then I arranged that encounter at the grocery store, and... here we are.

"I have to say, I'm very happy with my choice. Over the past few months, I have really enjoyed living in your body. I love when you take a shower, the way your abs feel under your hands when they're all slick with soap. I love the way you reach into your pockets when no one is watching and gently scrape your fingers against the sides of your balls. I've even enjoyed your workouts. Somehow the feel of muscles straining under a load of weights or burning during a run is a lot more enjoyable when it's your muscles doing the straining and not mine. And when you had sex... well, I was kind of turned off with all the breast-licking and such, but I always tuned in for the climax at the end. After all, an orgasm is an orgasm, right?"

Paul burned with such rage and humiliation that he was sure his head must explode from the pressure of his blood.

"Now, it's getting late, so let me tell you where we're going to go from here. Experiencing your senses was nice, but it's not enough. I need to have a little more say in what we do with that lovely body. But I'm not a completely heartless guy; after all, it was your body once. It wouldn't be fair of me to completely take over. So here's what's going to happen, Paul.

"You go back to your previous life. Good news, right? I got you into some trouble with your wife and your employer, but the damage is not irreparable. You can apologize profusely to each of them and maybe get back into each of their good graces. You can live your life just like you've been doing. Oh, and you can get yourself another car. Something practical this time, OK?

"All I'll ask for is two nights a week, let's say Wednesdays and

Saturdays, although I can be flexible if you need to switch days sometimes. On my nights, I'll take control. We'll most likely go to a bar, pick up a hot guy, and have my kind of sex. You can watch if you want, or if you'd rather, I'll turn off your senses and you can pretend it isn't happening. Sometimes, we'll skip the bar scene and I'll bring you here so you and I can get it on in private.

"Every once in a while, maybe once or twice a month, I'll want to do some heavier stuff, though. Stuff like you did this afternoon. Are you into S&M, Paul? I thought not. I am. I like to give pain and I like to receive it. It felt so good when you were hanging there in that dungeon, stretched out tight with those weights yanking on your balls and your tits and that whip kissing your flesh..." Fillmore trailed off, his eyes unfocused and dreamy-looking.

"I won't get you into anything that would cause you permanent damage, of course," he continued. "your body is too perfect for me to allow it to be disfigured.

"So, that's the plan: I get your body two nights a week. But the plan is only good for as long as you co-operate with me. If you give me any hint of a reason to suspect that you're trying to get out of our arrangement, then your liberty is canceled and we go to Plan B. Plan B is: I get you full time. You give up your job, your home, and any chance of seeing your wife or friends again and you stay here with me. You spend your days doing chores for me, keeping my house clean, cooking, that sort of thing, and exercising faithfully to keep that flawless body in top shape. You exist to serve my needs.

"I'll use you hard, both for sex and for pain. I could easily spend years exploring all the possibilities that our linked nerve-nets provide us. Here's one idea - I think you'd look really good with pierced nipples. Maybe I'll have you pierce them yourself. Or have you give yourself a tattoo. Maybe even a brand. Wouldn't that be wild, to have you hold a white-hot branding iron against your own chest? I tell you, the idea of watching you torture yourself and being able to feel what you feel as you do it turns me on so much I almost can't stand it.

"And there's more to come. I don't have the capability to do it yet, but one of the things I'm working on is a way to record your sensations. Think about it - I could have a hot sex-and-torture session with you and record every sensation your body feels. Then I could play it back for you, over and over and over! You - and I - would get to experience all of the joy and pain multiple times but with no risk of damaging your perfect body.

"Oh, the nerve net provides so many possibilities. Have you ever thought what it would be like to live in a mirror world? I could leave all your sensory input the same, but flip your motor output left-to-right. Everything you tried to do with your right hand would actually be done by your left, and vice versa. I wonder how long it would take you to get used to that? Days, maybe? Then, once you did, I'd flip you back to normal. Or maybe screw you up worse - you know, hook your biceps up to your calves, your toes to your lips and watch you try to cope."

"There are all kinds of ways I can mess with you. With enough processing power I could arrange to have myself edited out of your visual field in real time. I would be totally invisible to you. Man, I tell you, the possibilities are just endless."

The full horror of what Fillmore was capable of became abundantly clear to Paul. He sought desperately for some escape from this madman but his body remained stubbornly immobile in its seat.

"And there's always sex, of course. I don't know what turns me on more, the idea of fucking your hot, tight ass or the knowledge that you'll hate every minute of it. It'll be so hot to see what it feels like to experience both your sensations and my own as I ram into you, or you ram into me. I'll need a lot more practice to get to the point where I can control your body and mine at the same time, but when I can do it, the sex will be just incredible.

Fillmore's voice trailed off as he lost himself again in his fantasies. Paul's body waited patiently, like a horse hitched up outside a saloon with nothing to do but wait for its master to return with more orders for it to follow.

"But I digress. Anyway, that's Plan B. That's what will happen to you if you try to resist me in any way. Try to tell anyone what I've done to you, try to thwart me at all, and you will instantly forfeit your right to continue your own life. Is that clear?"

Paul nodded, then looked down at his lap. The front of his pants was still tented out by his jutting erection, now more than half an hour old and starting to ache dully. He longed to shift position to ease the discomfort, but was still unable to move from the neck down. Fillmore noticed Paul's distress, and the cause for it.

"Whoops. Silly me," said Fillmore. "How careless I can be sometimes. Let's take care of that, shall we? Simon says 'you can come now.'"

Paul did.

"Anne Marie, can I talk to you about something?"

"What is it, Adam?" Anne Marie answered.

There was no one else around, but Adam still kept his voice low. "This is very intrusive of me," he said, "and if you want me to mind my own business, just say so. But I have to ask. How are things with Paul?"

Anne Marie froze for a moment, then exploded. "I could not *possibly* care less how that psychotic nut case is doing. Quite honestly, after the way he treated me, I hope I never see the lunatic again."

Adam stepped back from the force of her anger.

"If you had any idea how that bastard behaved... I'm so furious I can barely see straight. He... no, never mind, I don't want to get into it. But I'll tell you this, he'll never *ever* do it again."

"Okay, okay, forget I said anything." He turned to go, then looked back. "But since you mention lunacy, I saw Paul on Friday. He was acting very strangely, almost like he was a completely different..."

Anne Marie held up her hand. "Stop. I truly do not care. If it's something to do with Paul, it's none of my concern. We're through. Whatever he did, whatever he does from now on, it has nothing to do with me."

"Right. Okay. Well, I'll see you later..."

Anne Marie was still seething when he left. Part of her knew that making Adam the target of her anger was unfair. He was just the messenger, after all. No, not even a messenger, more of an innocent bystander. It was Paul who was really the focus of her wrath. She knew that in two or three hours, or perhaps tomorrow, when she had cooled down a bit, she would go to Adam and apologize for snapping at him.

For now, though, she was too full of fury.

Still, that same part of her couldn't help but wonder... had he been about to say "a completely different person?"

Interesting. Because that was exactly how she would have described the new psychotic Paul. Perhaps after she apologized she would ask him what he had been going to say.

But not now.

Paul found that putting his life back together was a mixed bag. Some damage was easy to repair, some not so easy.

Over the weekend, he sent his employer a message saying he wanted to request a meeting first thing Monday morning to apologize for his outburst. During his apology, he explained how distraught he had been over his wife's departure the night before and offered assurances that such behavior would not happen again. His employer guardedly accepted his explanation and by mid-morning, Paul was back at work.

Getting a new car was even easier. He went online to order an off-the-shelf GM-Toyota box on Saturday morning, and by sundown it had been delivered to his driveway. Paul figured there was no sense in getting another Jaguar as long as Fillmore's machines were in his body, so a simple point-A-to-point-B car would do fine. Being able to use the grid lanes on the freeway even shaved four minutes off his commute.

Repairing his marriage, on the other hand, was too difficult to even consider. He didn't even try to talk to Anne Marie. Instead, he left her a message saying that he loved her desperately but that he had some issues he needed to attend to before he would jeopardize her safety by being in her presence again. As soon as he had worked things out, he would contact her.

Wednesday night rolled around. Paul came home early from work to ensure that whatever was going to happen to him happened in the privacy of his home. He kicked around the house for over two hours, watching CNN without hearing a word of it and eating something he couldn't remember five minutes later. Around eight o'clock, Fillmore used Paul's mouth to say "OK, I'm ready to go. Do you want to watch, or should I turn you off?"

As disgusted as Paul was at the thought of participating in more gay sex, he was more terrified at the prospect of being thrust into black nothingness again, this time for hours, and so he chose to stay present. Besides, he might learn something about weaknesses in Fillmore's net by observing.

Fillmore drove him to a gay bar where he spent four hours drinking and dancing. Guys cruised him constantly, and Paul thought that Fillmore must be in heaven with so many offers to choose from that he could afford to turn down the first five guys who came on to him. With the sixth, though, he sidled off to a back room and got his dick sucked.

It wasn't bad, actually. The guy was an excellent cocksucker. He got down on his knees while Paul stood leaning against a wall. He pulled open Paul's pants and eased the long, thick erection out of its confinement. Then he engulfed the entire length with his warm mouth, taking it deeper than Paul would have thought anyone could. Paul gasped as the man's throat muscles massaged the sensitive tip while his tongue lapped against the shaft and his hands worked and kneaded Paul's ballsac.

The sensations were just too overwhelming. It was over in minutes. Paul felt his groin tighten and his balls pull up toward his belly. The man took a quick gasp for air then plunged back down. Paul's cock erupted, spurting out what felt like an enormous load, although it was impossible to be sure how big because every drop disappeared down his anonymous partner's greedy throat. They parted wordlessly, and Paul went back for more dancing and drinking.

Later on, he returned to the back room, this time with two different men, one thin, tall, and sandy-haired, the other short, dark, and very heavily muscled. The experience was not nearly so enjoyable the second time around. This time, he was the one doing the sucking, and being on the other end of the dick was far less pleasant for him.

He was positioned on his belly on top of a block-shaped cushion. The blond was sitting naked in front of him with his legs spread and his crotch squarely in Paul's face. His sweaty groin smelled repugnant to Paul, but Fillmore was obviously not bothered a bit, because he lowered Paul's mouth to the cock in front of it and opened wide to take it in.

Paul felt the penis enter his mouth, sliding against his tongue and forcing its way to the back of his throat. He would have gagged if he could. Instead, his hand reached out to wrap around the shaft and he began to pump up and down in time with the movements of his head. Without any experience in the matter, he had no way to judge if the performance he was delivering was as good as what he had received earlier. Fillmore must have known his stuff, though, because the object of his attentions began to moan and grunt contentedly.

As bad as the cock down his throat was, though, worse was what was happening behind him. The dark muscleman grabbed Paul's upturned ass with his meaty hands and spread the cheeks apart. The next sensation Paul felt took Paul so by surprise that he couldn't even guess what it was he was feeling. Then he realized that it was the man's tongue snaking out of his mouth and into Paul's asshole. Another wave of revulsion washed over him, but there was no stopping the action.

Insistently, the tongue flicked and probed and forced its way through the tight opening. It hurt less on entering than the cocks of several days earlier had, but it was still a sickening violation. Even though it wasn't his tongue doing the probing, Paul couldn't stop imagining the action in reverse. As bad as it was to have a dick in his mouth, how much worse would it be to plunge his tongue into some stranger's ass, lapping up the filth while the stench filled his nose?

His stomach clenching, he determinedly tried to think about anything else while the action heated up. It was hard to distract himself completely - Fillmore seemed to think Paul didn't need to breathe quite as often as Paul wanted to. He tended to hold the blond's cock firmly in Paul's throat for several seconds past the point where Paul would have pulled himself off to gasp for air. Paul felt his head spinning a bit from the lack of oxygen.

The tongue behind him, meanwhile, was soon replaced with the muscleman's dick. With Fillmore in charge, the entry went much more easily than it had in the dungeon, and the man was soon humping away. Each thrust forced Paul toward the blond and the three of them were soon caught up in their rhythm. Fillmore caused Paul's hand to wander down to his cock, where he began to stroke himself off.

The blond came first. Thick, sticky semen squirted into Paul's mouth. Fillmore swallowed some of it, but more dripped out and coated Paul's lips and face. Paul was next, leaving a puddle on the cushion under his belly. The muscleman took a good while longer. Paul found the fucking much harder to take after his own orgasm had dissipated. The discomfort was magnified, somehow, and Paul was just desperate for it to be over. At long last, the man finally reached his peak. A few more frantic thrusts and the pounding subsided. He slipped out with a wet slurp and Paul felt a trail of slime trickle down the inside of his thigh.

Between this experience and the last, Paul had never felt so used, so humiliated, so violated in his entire life. Fillmore drove him home and left him. He spent at least an hour in a very hot shower and yet still didn't feel clean when he was through.

The next Saturday, Fillmore took Paul to a leather club. At one point in the evening, Paul found himself strapped to a padded X-shaped frame, held upright while a leather flogger was applied to his back, ass, and thighs. Later on, he was the one doing the flogging while a muscular Latino writhed enthusiastically under his ministrations. He spent a long stretch of time atop a low platform, chained up on his hands and knees, butt to butt with the same Latino. They had their balls roped together so that every time one of them moved forward he pulled on both sets of nuts. They were each compelled to orally service a series of cocks that paraded past them in a seemingly endless supply.

That night, when he was back in his home, the ache in his groin and the sticky semen that he couldn't seem to wash completely off his chin only served to further inflame Paul's cold rage. The situation was intolerable. His chin grew red and raw as he scrubbed and scrubbed at the dried cum and swore that one day he would get his freedom. And after that, his revenge.

As the days passed by, Anne Marie became less and less sure what had happened between her and Paul, and began to wonder if her response was really what it should have been.

She had apologized to Adam the day after lashing out at him, but he had been reluctant to tell her anything concrete about Paul beyond that he was "acting strange." She had wanted to press him for details, but then Linda came by to say that the layout for the Listerine campaign had to be completely redone and they were all suddenly up to their ears in overtime. Then on Wednesday Doreen had quit which only made things worse. There just wasn't time to find Adam for a talk.

Now the weekend had come and she finally had time to think.

Throughout their courtship and marriage, Paul had never treated her with anything but courtesy and respect. She knew he had a wilder side that came out when he competed, whether the competition was at work or simply playing basketball. But with her, he was never anything but a gentleman.

It was as though she had been dragged up the stairs and nearly raped by someone who looked like Paul but really wasn't. In the week that had passed since she had left the house to stay with Catherine, she had had a lot of time to think about what had happened. And the more she thought, the more she regretted her hasty departure.

She had always known that she had a hot temper. She could fly into a rage in a heartbeat and then cool down again equally quickly, sometimes regretting things she had said or done in her anger. It had always been part of her nature, a part that she had mostly learned to keep under control. Mostly. Perhaps this was one of the times when she had allowed her emotions to run away too quickly. On cooler reflection, it didn't make sense to throw away the three years of their marriage, not to mention two more of friendship and dating, without at least trying to salvage things.

With that in mind, she tried to talk to Paul. He refused to take her calls. She linked him at home, at work, on his mobile, but could only reach his messenger software to leave messages that he never returned. And when she stopped by the house in person, she discovered it had been reprogrammed to refuse her access.

And it wasn't just her, it seemed. When she asked around, she learned that Paul appeared to be cutting everyone out of his life. Friends, family, and co-workers all said that his behavior toward them had turned polite but distant.

She couldn't figure it out. Yet. But her interest was now piqued, and she wanted to know what was going on. And when she wanted something, she could be as tenacious as a bulldog.

Despite Fillmore's threat of permanent enslavement as punishment for rebellion, the current situation was unacceptable. Paul refused to concede that he would have to remain under Fillmore's control indefinitely. There had to be a way to break free. Paul was a bright, aggressive guy. He would try to remember everything that Fillmore had said about how the net worked, probing for its limitations and weaknesses, and he was certain he could eventually find a way out.

It was a challenging task. While it was not physically possible for Fillmore to be snooping on him at every single moment, there was no way for Paul to know when he was being watched and when he wasn't. Thus, he had to assume that everything he did was monitored. He also had to assume that even though Fillmore had access to his senses, the creep couldn't read his thoughts. Otherwise, any plans he made would be doomed from the start.

After weeks of intense thought, Paul finally decided on the plan that seemed to give the best chance of winning his escape from Fillmore's grip.

The idea came to him as he was rooting around in the medicine cabinet for something to take the edge off the pain after a Wednesday night session at Fillmore's home. His balls ached fiercely after the punishment his own hands had administered to them. He found some Tylenol and in the process of looking came across a bottle of Darvocet left over from when he had had a cracked tooth repaired the previous year. Paul remembered that the Darvocet had not only taken the pain away, but also knocked him out. Trying hard not to pay attention to the bottle, he hoped it hadn't lost its potency after so much time.

His break came three weeks after that. He overheard Sharla, one of his co-workers, talking about the ski trip to Utah she, her husband, and their three teenagers would be taking. With five people plus ski gear, they were renting a trailer to pull behind their car. Sharla's husband would be picking her up with the trailer from work Friday afternoon.

Friday morning, Paul slipped three of the Darvocet pills out of the bottle while he was brushing his teeth and dropped them into his pocket. Lingering in the office common area around four o'clock that afternoon, he heard Sharla's husband call her to say he was on his way. Paul went back to his office and dry-swallowed the three tablets. He waited for a few seconds, but there was no reaction from Fillmore. So far, so good.

As Sharla headed for the elevators about fifteen minutes later, Paul wrapped up his work for the day and joined her, already starting to feel drowsy. They made idle chit-chat during the descent to the underground parking garage, and Paul walked her to her waiting car.

Once she was in, he slipped around to the back of the trailer. It was not large, but it was completely enclosed with a roof and a door. As the car started to pull away, Paul yanked open the trailer door, leaped inside, and pulled the door shut behind him. There was barely enough room for him amid all the luggage. He made himself as comfortable as he could as the drug pulled at him with its lure of oblivion.

Paul dared to hope for a moment. He was in a vehicle that was moving inexorably east. In moments, his body would be unconscious and unable to be used against his will. There was nothing Fillmore could do to prevent Paul's escape.

Of course, getting away from Fillmore was just the first step. Once he was out of range he would take the next step of finding a doctor who would believe his story and help him to get the infection of nanomachines removed. And when his body was fully his own once again, it would be time for step three: revenge.

That thought brought a smile to Paul's face as he allowed the Darvocet to carry his consciousness away.

"Adam, can we talk?"

"Sure, Anne Marie," Adam answered. She could see that he was wary, and didn't blame him a bit. She resolved once again to try to keep her temper under better control.

"Would you mind if we went into the conference room? This space is kind of open."

He followed her down the hallway and into the smaller of the art department's two conference rooms. She shut the door behind them.

"You came to me a few weeks ago," she said, "and wanted to tell me something about Paul. I snapped at you, which I am very sorry for. I was pretty overwrought at the time, which is not an excuse, just an explanation. But I'm much calmer now, and I really would like to know what you were going to say."

"I don't know, Anne Marie," said Adam. "You may have said it in anger, but I think you had a good point - now that you two have separated, what Paul does is his own business."

"But that's just why I'm asking," she said. "I'm starting to wonder if Paul is really himself. I've been trying to talk to him for almost a month, but he refuses to speak to me. And it's not just me - his sister, his co-workers, his friends all say that he's pretty much cut them off. I'm beginning to wonder if he's ill or something. Maybe he needs help, some kind of intervention, but is too macho to ask for it. So anything you can tell me might help me figure out what's going on. Please?"

Adam relented. "All right. But this is probably going to be hard for you to hear."

Anne Marie was resolute. "Go ahead."

"Well, I saw him a few weeks ago. He was behaving very strangely. I don't think he recognized me. Not that I would expect him to - he only met me that one time at the Christmas party two years ago. But - and this is where it gets strange - he was at a leather club in San Francisco. A gay leather club."

"A gay leather club?" Anne Marie echoed. "That's strange indeed. Paul is most definitely not gay. He's even... well, not exactly homophobic, but certainly homo-tense. An attitude which, as you know, I do not share."

"I know," said Adam, "and I appreciate that. But that's what I thought about Paul, at least until I saw him there. I got this very odd vibe from him. He acted almost schizophrenic, like there were two very different personalities inside one body. One Paul brought him into this club, made a... well, a challenge to the guys who were there, then vanished. Then the other Paul took over and did what I would have expected him to do - tried to get the hell out. Only by then he couldn't."

"What do you mean he couldn't?"

"Are you sure you want to hear? I mean, the details are pretty graphic."

Anne Marie fixed him with her dark stare. "Adam, I'm working under the assumption that my husband has gone insane. He has completely cut me out of his life, and all he's told me is that he 'has issues to deal with,' which is so vague it's meaningless - anything from an affair to a gambling addiction to cancer. What I need to know is whether I should try to intervene or just give up. So tell me - it all this just because he has suddenly discovered his inner fairy? Or is there something more going on?"

Adam told her what he had seen, holding nothing back.

"... and just like that, as soon as I set him loose, straight Paul was gone and sex-pig Paul was back. It was like flipping a switch. Even his voice was different. When he was tied down, screaming and yelling, he talked one way. But when the restraints were off, he spoke differently. His voice was more nasal and his vowels were flatter, like they way they talk in the Midwest. It was creepy seeing the change. There is definitely something weird going on with him. I mean, I only met the guy once, but even I could see that."

Anne Marie sat and thought for a long while before speaking again.

"Wow," she said, finally. "That's a lot to digest. What you've just described is so completely unlike the Paul I know that if I hadn't seen his odd behavior myself there is no chance I would have believed your story. It's just unreal. But there's got to be some explanation. I just can't think what."

"Well, ordinarily I'd say the simplest explanation is the most likely," said Adam. "There are an awful lot of straight married guys out there who still manage to find time to walk on the other side of the street every so often. Usually, they're happy with their wives and want to stay married, so they keep their gay trysts secret. It can go on for years. I see it all the time. But this doesn't fit that pattern. The gay married guys want to have it both ways, but Paul drove you away, not to mention all his family and friends. Is he trying to go gay full time and is pulling away from everyone he knows out of shame? Maybe. But then, why the weird split personality thing? I don't know what to make of it. Maybe you're right and he is going crazy."

"Maybe so. Maybe so."

"Listen, Anne Marie, I'll be happy to talk more about this if you want, but I've got to get back to work."

"Of course. Thank you, Adam."

Paul awoke slowly. His senses came back to him bit by bit as the effects of the drug wore off. He gradually became aware of rumbling, of jostling, of coolness. He thought he could have moved if he had wanted to, but there didn't seem to be any need. His job was not to take action, but merely to wait patiently. Events would unfold as they would.

Time passed.

Then, with a snap, Paul came to full alertness. Immediately, a wave of disorientation washed over him and his stomach clenched. One glance was enough to tell him he was no longer in Sharla's trailer, but he couldn't tell exactly where he was. It was a room of some kind, but everything in it seemed to spin wildly around. Nothing stayed still long enough for him to look at it. Perhaps this was a lingering effect of the Darvocet? It hadn't happened when he took the drug for his tooth, but then, he hadn't taken three pills at once then, either.

He shut his eyes to close off the chaos, but the spinning continued, and in fact, grew even worse. It felt like he was floating in space; he could sense neither up nor down.

Taking a deep breath, Paul tried to calm down and focus on what he could. He was sitting on a hard, flat surface. A chair, perhaps? Tentatively, he opened his eyes again and lowered his head to look. He promptly overbalanced and fell forward off the chair onto a bare concrete floor. He lay there twitching while the first hint of panic tickled his neck hairs. The world would not stop spinning.

"Hello, Paul," Fillmore's voice said. Paul's skin crawled. The sound came from above him and to his right. He turned to look but he still couldn't seem to focus his eyes. Every time he tried to look at something, his field of view spun even more crazily.

"I'm a little disappointed that you tried to escape me," Fillmore said. "But in a way, I'm happy, too. Because now we can end this little farce of shared custody over your body."

Paul rolled around on the floor. He kept trying to get up but his body behaved like it was drunk. He could not coordinate his movements enough to get up to his knees, let alone stand.

"You're feeling disoriented," Fillmore went on, "because I've shut off your inner ear's sense of balance. I've also reversed your eyes. Left is right and right is left and your brain is having trouble processing the information it's receiving. Every time you try to move your eyes inward to focus on something close up, they spread out to the sides instead, and vice versa. Given time, you might learn to adapt, but for now, I think it effectively keeps you out of trouble. And it's so much more fun than simply immobilizing you, don't you think?"

Paul screamed his terror and frustration. When his screams

tapered off to moans and whimpers, Fillmore continued.

"Paul, I have to tell you that your little plan almost worked. I had grown careless because things had been going so well for so long, and I wasn't paying as much attention to you as I should have been. The car you were in got all the way past Vallejo before I even noticed you were away. Shame on me.

"But I do like to prepare for many contingencies. One feature of your nerve net that I didn't bother to share with you is that it is capable of connecting to the freeway grids. The bandwidth is narrow, so I can't send and receive much data that way, but it's enough for blunt work. By the time I noticed you were gone, you were out of range of the Bay Area grid, but once you got near Sacramento, their grid picked you up. When the car slowed for a crowded merge ramp, you got out of the trailer and made your way to a nearby strip mall. You sat there until I came and picked you up, calm and sleepy from the drug you took and the chemicals my net stimulated your body to produce.

"The drug, by the way, was totally ineffective. Your own brain was knocked out, but not my net. You should have anticipated that. You would have had more success if you had handcuffed yourself to the frame of the trailer and thrown the key out of reach. Still, your effort was a good one, and if you had stayed away from the cities, you would have made your escape."

Fillmore leaned down close to where Paul lay on the floor. Two enormous copies of the jowly, acne-scarred face floated and pulsated in Paul's vision.

"Paul," he said, "you can be sure I will never, ever be that careless again." The voice echoed nastily in Paul's ears. Paul shut his eyes and struggled to turn away, but only succeeded in cracking his skull against the floor.

Even as he reeled with dizziness, he could feel his body rising up. It moved confidently, smoothly, despite the chaos in his mind.

He felt himself pull all his clothing off until the cool air caressed his naked skin. He then walked to the wall. Every movement sent more waves of nausea and dizziness coursing through him, but the deliberate movements of his body were unaffected.

He took some leather cuffs from a rack that was hanging on the wall. He carefully buckled the cuffs around his ankles and wrists, then backed up to an empty stretch of wall. Still moving calmly, he clipped both ankle cuffs to rings set in the concrete floor, spreading his legs wide apart. Then he reached up high over his head and hooked one of the wrist cuffs to a similar bolt waiting there.

He couldn't reach to attach his other hand, so Fillmore came over to do it, leaving Paul's body spread wide open and vulnerable. Fillmore wheeled over a tray covered with various objects. Paul still could not get his eyes to focus correctly and so could not see exactly what the implements were. He only caught glimpses in the light from the bare bulb overhead. Strips of black leather. Wires. White rope. Gleaming metal.

Fillmore's face loomed once more in his kaleidoscope vision. He began to fiddle with Paul's exposed genitals, wrapping and tugging and stretching and taping while Paul tried without success to see what was going on. Fully in control of his body once again - little good that it did him - Paul frantically pulled on his restraints and bellowed his despair. When the first blast of current shot through his testicles it felt like he had been kicked there. His entire body tried to fold in on itself, but the cuffs held him firmly in place.

"Mmmm," moaned Fillmore, massaging his own groin. "That burns soooooo good! I just love getting my balls zapped."

Paul felt Fillmore's body move close to his. Chill, flabby skin pressed against his own, and the smell of stale grease and unwashed flesh filled his nose. Fillmore's erect penis rubbed against his thigh. Paul groaned.

"Aw, what's the matter, Paul?" Fillmore purred in his ear. He sent another brief jolt through the wires. Both men spasmed in response and Paul choked out another grunt.

"Come on, take it like a man," Fillmore chided. "After all, this hurts me exactly as much as it hurts you."

Paul howled.

"I need you to do me a favor," Anne Marie said. She had commandeered the conference room again.

"What's that?" asked Adam.

"I need you to pick up my husband."

"Excuse me? Somehow I don't think you mean in the physical, lift-him-off-the-ground sense."

"Correct. See, I had a thought. You said that when Paul got to the leather bar, he was acting weird. 'Sex-pig' Paul, you called him. But when he was tied up, he acted more like the real Paul. Then when the ropes came off the sex pig took over again. So I want you to pick him up, take him home, and tie him up. Maybe the real Paul will come through and you can ask him what the hell is going on."

"That's a real long shot," said Adam. "I mean, just because it happened once, there's no guarantee it'll work that way again. Maybe he's gotten over the whole guilt thing and there's only one Paul now. Or maybe he's stopped cruising the gay bars. I only saw him that once, you know, and that was a long time ago. Believe me, I'd have noticed if I'd seen him again. He may not be out there for me to pick up."

"Oh, I'm pretty sure he is," said Anne Marie, "and I can even tell you which bars to look in. Listen to this - Paul may have locked me out physically, but I was able to access the house AI remotely.

I told it to record anything Paul said when he was in the house alone. This is what I got. It's from yesterday evening."

She clicked a button on her computer screen and Paul's voice came out of the speaker.

"All right, you bastard, are you there? What's it going to be tonight?"

"I think we'll hit Skyboy's first, then swing on over to Tartarus." The voice was Paul's, but the inflection was strange, different from his normal style of speech. Just as Adam had said, the sound was more nasal, with flat Midwestern vowels and a hint of whininess. Though this was at least the tenth time she had played the clip, it was still disconcerting to Anne Marie's ears.

"Ah, shit, I was afraid you'd say that. You know I hate that pit."

"Of course you do. Hey, I could always turn you off if you'd rather..."

"No. Fuck. Leave me plugged in. All right. You want me to go get changed by myself, or are you going to do it?"

"I got it."

The clip ended.

"Play it again," said Adam, leaning forward with his head cocked. They listened to it a second time through, then a third.

Anne Marie said "Is that not one of the strangest monologues you ever heard? I don't think we could ask for any better evidence that there's something odd going on. Now, Paul won't let me get near him, but as far as he's concerned, you're just another guy to... well, you're just another guy. He doesn't seem aware of the connection between you and me. You'll have to be my eyes and ears and hands, Adam. All you have to do is get through to the real Paul."

"Oh, that's all, is it? You make it sound so simple." Adam pondered a while, then said "Jeez, he's hanging out at Tartarus? That place really is a pit. I mean, I like to get rough and dirty sometimes, but those guys make me look like a choirboy. Your hubby is getting himself into some seriously kinky stuff."

"Not for much longer if I can help it."

"And you really want me to tie him up? Pardon my indelicacy here, but should I fuck him, too?"

"If necessary, yes," said Anne Marie. "He's apparently having sex with anonymous strangers, so why not someone I know and trust? You have my blanket permission to do whatever you need to do to help me figure out what's going on."

"OK, I just wanted to be sure. All right, I'll do it. But I have to tell you, this is one of the oddest favors anyone has ever asked me for."

"Thank you, Adam."

The bar was crowded. Glistening shirtless bodies jerked and jumped on the dance floor to the insistent thrum of the music. Strobe lights flashed and the air was filled with the smell of liquor and male sweat.

Paul took another pull of his vodka tonic. This was his first night out since his failed escape attempt a week earlier. It had not been a pleasant seven days, and his body had the marks to prove it. His back still burned from a series of floggings - Fillmore certainly loved the crack of leather against bare skin. Muscles all over his body ached from the punishing workouts he had been driven through. And his right nipple was tender though it had been almost a week since Fillmore had made him pierce it. Fillmore had a habit of idly fingering the barbell-shaped stud through Paul's shirt, which would have made Paul wince each time if he had had any control over his facial muscles.

But now Friday night had rolled around, and bruises or no, Fillmore wanted to go out clubbing. So far tonight, Paul had watched him turn down four unspoken invitations from guys on their way to the back rooms, as well as another more explicit offer. Paul was getting used to the pattern. He was even developing an eye for the kind of men that turned Fillmore on. He figured Fillmore would most likely wait another ten minutes or so, long enough to finish the drink, then head to the back with some guy who had a body with powerful, sculpted muscles and not a lot of hair. A body very much like Paul's.

At least it was just Skyboy's tonight, Paul thought. A regular gay bar and not a bondage club. He was finding that he was getting better at handling the man-on-man sex, but he didn't think he would ever be able to cope with the bondage and the pain that got Fillmore off.

"Hey, Paul."

Paul turned to look at the man who had spoken to him. He was leaning on the bar next to where Paul stood, eying him up and down. He almost fit Fillmore's type, lean and tall, though his hair was shaggier than Fillmore preferred and his physique could use a tad more definition. Paul figured Fillmore would blow him off, but the fact that the guy knew his name apparently intrigued him.

"Adam," the man said. "Remember me? I gave you a lift after you decided you didn't want your Jaguar any more?"

"Right," Paul heard himself say. "Yeah, I remember."

"Good. I'm glad you do. 'Cause I was wondering if you also remember what else went on that day. I sure do. It's funny. You look like this total top-stud, but I saw you in action. I know that underneath that tough-guy exterior there lurks a serious pain pig." Adam reached over and tweaked Paul's chest piercing in the same way Fillmore had been.

Paul watched Adam's face. He could tell Fillmore was mulling over the implied offer. Paul prayed that he would decline. *Please, let it be just sex tonight.* When he didn't respond right away, Adam continued.

"My place is not far away. Just a few blocks. It's very well equipped. Of course, there's only one of me, so I can't provide you with the gang-bang you enjoyed so much before. Even so, I think we could still manage to have ourselves a good time."

Paul downed the rest of his drink, then took Adam by the arm and guided him outside.

Adam's place was indeed well equipped. Paul cringed at the sight of some of the equipment he saw in the basement. He had experienced a lot of bondage and torture since Fillmore took him over, but no matter how often it happened, it never seemed to get any easier. Paul resigned himself to yet another several-hours-long session of pain and abuse ending with yet another cock shoved up his ass or down his throat.

"This way," Adam said. He guided Paul to a table. Fillmore started to take Paul's clothes off, but Adam stopped him, saying "Not just yet."

Paul lay down on the table and Adam buckled him securely in place. Leather straps went across his chest, waist, hips, thighs, and ankles, pinning him down to the table. Adam tightened the straps and then attached more restraints. Tape and ropes went over Paul's hands and fingers, feet and toes until the only thing Paul could move was his head.

"There," said Adam. "That should do it."

Then, he turned the lights out and left.

Paul was surprised. Usually the scenes got started right away. Fillmore seemed surprised, too. He called Adam's name a few times, but there was no response. Eventually he gave up.

There was nothing to do.

The position was not uncomfortable. The table was covered with leather padding, so there was no hard surface pressing against his skin. The restraints prevented him from changing position, but even that was not too bad. Paul usually slept on his back anyway. He kept waiting for something to happen, but nothing did. With nothing to see and only the soft sound of the ventilation system to hear, Paul's head began to grow fuzzy. He didn't think he ever actually slept, but he did drift in and out of a dreamlike twilight state.

Then, suddenly, he was awake and alert. Tentatively, he tried his voice. "Help?" he whispered. He had control! Fillmore must have fallen asleep and left him. His mind raced, trying to think of how to use the opportunity.

Instantly, Adam was at his side.

"Paul?" he whispered back.

"Yes. Please, please help me. I'm not really..."

"I know. I know who you really are, and I want to help you. What can you tell me?"

Paul told him everything he could about Fillmore and the nanomachines. It only took minutes, but Paul was petrified that Fillmore would swoop in at any moment and seize control again.

When he had finished, Adam said "OK. Now I know what we're up against. It's a far-fetched story, but it certainly fits what I've seen.

"Now, I'm going to work out a plan to get you free of him, but for tonight, I'm afraid we still have to go through with the scene. If we don't, your parasite will know something is wrong and he won't meet with me again. But if we make it good, he'll be so eager for a repeat performance that he'll walk right into whatever trap I set up."

"Who are you?" asked Paul.

"Never mind," said Adam. "The less you know, the less Fillmore can learn."

"Just be careful," Paul said. "This guy can shut down my heart and lungs in a second if he chooses to. Whatever your plan is, be ready for him to fight back."

"I know. I will. Tell me, what does Fillmore like? What can I do to you tonight that will make him hungry to come back for more?"

"Whips. He loves getting whipped. And he likes having things shoved up his ass. Ball pain turns him on, too."

"But not you," said Adam.

Paul actually laughed. "Hell, no! But like the old saying goes, I'd gladly give my left nut if it will help me get rid of him for good!"

Adam chuckled softly. "I don't think we'll have to go that far, but I do need to make it convincing. Don't worry - I'm very good at this. It'll hurt like hell for now, but you won't have so much as a bruise in the morning. OK, here goes."

Adam stepped back and snapped the lights on, shouting "WAKE UP, YOU LAZY SON OF A BITCH!" He came forward to where Paul lay and slapped his face back and forth. "C'MON, WAKE UP! UP, UP, UP! I DIDN'T BRING YOU HERE SO YOU COULD GET YOUR BEAUTY REST! GET UP!"

Paul felt a moment of disorientation as the bright light stabbed into his eyes, then the familiar feeling of trying to move a muscle and the lack of response that meant Fillmore had taken control.

The rest of the night passed as expected. Paul endured the most intense flogging of his life, suspended from the ceiling by his wrists with his legs wrapped around a support pole. Upon removing his shirt and seeing the marks underneath, Adam let out a low whistle and said "Man, you really do get into this, don't you?" Fillmore just begged him to lay it on.

Throughout the evening, various objects of steadily increasing diameter were forced into Paul's ass. His balls were pulled, slapped, twisted, squeezed, and crushed while he yowled his distress. He spent twenty minutes hanging again from his wrists while his rock-hard abdominal muscles were used as a punching bag for Adam's gloved fists.

Yet somehow, this episode was different from all those that had gone before. The unexpected surprise of hope somehow made the punishment easier to take. Not enjoyable, of course, the way it was for Fillmore. But bearable. Paul pictured it as like the pain of a long run or a grueling workout session - something he could work through; a means to an end.

The scene finally ended with Paul flat on his back. He hung suspended in a sling with his legs in the air while Adam corkscrewed his cock into Paul's ass. Adam was kind enough to jerk Paul off while he was thrusting, and the two of them steadily neared their climaxes together as their bodies slammed into one another.

Paul was surprised to find himself not loathing the feeling of a cock in his ass quite so much as he had in the past. In fact, there were moments when he seemed to be actually enjoying the act. It was sometimes difficult to tell if his body's responses were his own or Fillmore's, but he knew the physical sensations he was feeling were genuine. And this time those sensations were almost... pleasurable. Perhaps it was the same euphoric high that had made the pain easier to take, or the knowledge that one day soon he would get his chance to take Fillmore down. Whatever the cause, he found himself actually getting into the action, pumping his hips and squeezing his ass muscles around Adam's cock.

They shot simultaneously. As he neared his climax, Paul's ass involuntarily clamped down around Adam's shaft, causing Adam's moans to double in intensity. They both lingered right at the edge for an infinite moment, then both gushers blew at once. Paul's seed sprayed out over his taut belly just as Adam pumped his hot juice deep inside. The two men grunted and groaned in chorus together while their orgasms dragged on for what felt like forever.

When it was over and Paul was released from the straps, Fillmore walked him out without so much as a "thanks" to Adam and steered him through the dark streets back to his basement cell. The whole walk home, Paul was glad he had no control over his face, because he didn't think he could keep himself from grinning.

"That's not possible," Anne Marie said.

"That's what he said," Adam replied. "A nanotech net paralleling his nervous system. And it makes sense - it explains all of his strange behavior."

"But it's so far ahead of any nanotech system I've ever heard about. This Fillmore guy must be some kind of genius."

"A twisted one, that's for sure," said Adam.

They sat in silence for a few minutes. Then Adam spoke again. "The question is: what do we do about it? Call the cops?"

Anne Marie thought for another long moment. "Not just yet. They wouldn't believe this. The only reason I'm even considering it is because I saw him with my own eyes. The police would just dismiss this as some kind of lover's spat. They would go for what you called the simplest explanation: Paul is finally exploring some long-buried homosexual tendencies. No, we leave the police out for now."

"What, then? We know where the guy lives. You want me to go beat the crap out of him?" Adam asked.

"Tempting. But not while he can hurt or even kill Paul by just thinking about it. No, what we do first is go find ourselves a nanotech expert."

Paul didn't see Adam the following night at the dance club Fillmore brought him to, nor at the leather club the next week. Each time Fillmore sent him out, Paul prayed that this would be the night when Adam would come to his rescue, but each time he returned disappointed.

The days in Fillmore's house took their toll on Paul, both physically and mentally. Paul was exercising more than he ever had in his life, leaving him constantly sore and tired. He protested to Fillmore that overworking muscles was not the way to develop them, and was even counterproductive if the goal was to keep Paul's body in superb shape. Fillmore just snorted with disdain.

Paul also spent a large chunk of each day in some kind of restraint. Sometimes the restraint was physical - ropes or straps or chains. Other times, it was something only the nerve net could produce, like the time Fillmore clamped Paul's fingers around his ankles and froze them in place. He then granted Paul control of all the rest of his muscles and watched and laughed at the sight of Paul trying to free himself from his own iron grip. Paul was unable to break it. The only thing that finally set him free was the exhaustion of his arm muscles. After hours of holding his fingers clamped, the muscles in his arms finally reached a point where even the untiring stimuli from the nerve net could not force them to contract any longer. For more hours afterward, Paul's hands were useless lumps that he could do nothing with until his muscles finally recovered their strength.

Worst of all were the sensory torments. Fillmore started experimenting with the possibilities of the nerve nets. As he had threatened to do, he mirror-reversed Paul's sensory nerves one morning but left his motor nerves alone. Then he spent the rest of the day toying with him. He would bring a lit cigarette, for example, to Paul's left hand. Paul would see and feel it on his other side and jerk his right hand away, which of course did nothing to stop the pain. As the day wore on, Fillmore got more and more creative with the setup, forcing Paul to navigate increasingly complicated mazes of hot or sharp objects while living in a mirror world. When Paul finally was allowed to sleep that night, his entire body was shaking with the physical and mental strain of the day's exertions.

After two weeks of such torments, the hope that had energized Paul after his session with Adam had begun to fade. Then one night - a Thursday, if Paul's count of the days was accurate - a familiar shape slid up next to him as he was bumping and grinding on the dance floor at Skyboy's.

"Wanna go another round?" Adam asked.

Fillmore didn't respond immediately but only continued dancing. Then, after a long enough pause to make Paul fear the worst, he jerked his head toward the exit and moved toward it. Adam followed, and Paul's heart leaped for joy in his chest.

He had no idea what to expect upon entering Adam's door. Whatever plan Adam may have set up, Paul could only watch and be ready for a moment when he was free of Fillmore's control.

The walk to Adam's place passed so quickly Paul barely noticed it. The two men descended the stairs to Adam's basement, Adam standing behind Paul and guiding him with a hand on his shoulder. When they were three steps from the bottom, Paul was horrified to feel his muscles tensing for a move he recognized from his aikido training. He grasped Adam's wrist and ducked down, using his body weight to pull Adam forward over his shoulder. As Adam was lifted off the staircase, Paul gave a yank that spun Adam's head downward and flipped his legs over his body. He landed heavily on his shoulders and lay dazed.

Paul pounded his fist into Adam's face three or four times for good measure, knocking the back of his head against the concrete floor, then grabbed him by the shoulders and dragged him up onto the bondage table that Paul had been strapped to the last time he was here. Before Adam could recover, Paul had him temporarily fixed in place with metal cuffs and began working on a more permanent tie-down.

Adam struggled, but was unable to pull himself free. "Fillmore?" he said. It wasn't really a question.

"Right in one, ace," said Fillmore, tightening a strap attached to Adam's ankle and stretching his leg out taut. Adam gave a few more exploratory tugs at his bonds but the metal was inescapable.

"How did you know?" Adam said.

"Well, it wasn't rocket science, sport."

"But that was really Paul talking. Last time. Wasn't it? It had to have been."

"Of course it was Paul talking. Your plan was surprisingly effective - I had indeed fallen asleep, and I didn't wake up until you started shouting and flashing the lights." Fillmore had finished stretching out Adam's other leg and began replacing the metal cuffs around Adam's wrists with leather ones attached to chains.

"But," Fillmore continued, "one of the things I've been working on is a way to record Paul's sensations so I can play them back for him. You know, so I can give him the sense that his balls are being crushed in a vise without having to risk his jewels by actually doing it. Well, more than once, that is. I haven't gotten to the point where it works yet - there are some technical issues I still have to overcome.

"But recording sounds is relatively easy. I figured out how to do that a while ago. Now I routinely store the last six hours of Paul's auditory input. After you and I had our little fuckfest last time, I thought I might go back and see if I had missed anything while I was sleeping and, whaddaya know, I hear you and Paul conspiring. How you even figured out that there was something to be suspicious of eludes me... for now. But I think I might manage to persuade you to share that information with me during the course of the evening.

"And by the way, Paul, I'm starting to grow very tired of your constant attempts to escape. Although I suppose I can't really complain too much. After all, one of the things that I love about you is your spunk. I think if I ever did succeed in breaking you down completely you would quickly become boring to me. I'm not sure you'd like the sort of amusements I'm liable to dream up if that happens."

Fillmore finished stretching Adam out on the table. His body was completely taut, with his arms high over his head. Fillmore made some adjustments to the supports, tilting Adam's feet down and his head up. When he was finished, Adam was held at a thirty-degree angle to horizontal with his weight partially supported by the cuffs around his wrists. Fillmore picked up a nearby utility knife and began to cut away Adam's jacket and shirt.

"So, by all means, keep fighting me," he said as he worked. "Although after tonight you'll have to do it without the help of your friend here, because, well, Adam just might not have the stamina for all the entertainments I have planned for him tonight."

Paul raged impotently inside while Adam's eyes widened in fear.

"Well, it just makes sense," said Fillmore. "I mean, this is a perfect opportunity for me. See, Adam, I'm not just a 'serious pain pig',

I've also got one hell of a streak of sadism. Only I never get to indulge my fantasies to their fullest extent because there's always the inconvenient problem that my victim wants to be alive and undamaged after the scene ends.

"But with you, Adam, it's a different story. You know about the... mmm... special relationship that Paul and I share. That knowledge can't be allowed to get out. I've got a very comfortable situation going here, and I'm not going to let you muck it up. So I'm afraid you've got to go. But I promise you this, I'll make sure that your final trip is a very stimulating one, and that it lasts a good long time."

"You'll be caught," said Adam. "So far you've gotten away with stealing Paul's life, but people have noticed his absence. You can't stay hidden forever, and a dead body will just make your punishment worse when you finally get nailed."

"Oh, Adam," said Fillmore, slapping Adam's flank with his open palm, "you poor, benighted thinker of little thoughts. *I'm* not going to get caught - *Paul* is. Eventually. And when he does, all I have to do is flush the nanos out of his body and there will be no link back to me. Of course, I'll have to guarantee his silence before I shut down the net. An unfortunate heart attack would be simple enough to arrange."

Adam didn't respond. His muscles were straining against the tension he was under, and his bare chest glistened with sweat despite the cool temperature of the basement. Fillmore snorted, then went to rummage in Adam's stockpile of equipment and pulled out some candles and lit them. Then he carefully arranged some long, thin metal barbecue skewers so that one end of each perched atop the flames.

"I wonder if you can guess what I'm planning to do with these," Fillmore told Adam. "While they're warming up, I am curious. I really would like to know what you had planned. Whatever it was seems to have been spectacularly unsuccessful. You didn't even call the cops?"

Adam sighed. "No. I thought about it, but I just couldn't see them believing my story. All I had in mind was a Faraday cage."

Fillmore whooped. "A Faraday cage? I have got to find myself some worthier opponents! This is like matching wits with a banana slug!"

Adam protested. "It would have blocked your communication. You wouldn't have been able to issue commands to Paul's net. I would have gotten him into the cage, then taken him to see a buddy of mine at St. Theresa's. He has access to their MRI machine. We would have blasted your bugs with an EMP."

"Gee," Fillmore pretended to consider the possibility, "you're right, an electromagnetic pulse would knock out the nanos without harming Paul's cells, but an MRI? An MRI machine provides a focused pulse to a specific target. Sure, you'd knock out a few thousand nanos with each pulse and with diligent effort you could probably even clear out a section the size of his head. But as soon as you moved on to the next section, the ones that were left would start reproducing to fill in the void. It would be like trying to swat a billion fast-breeding flies one at a time. You wouldn't have had a chance.

"Now come on. Be honest with me. Unless you're a lot smarter than you've acted so far then I'm amazed that you can even pronounce 'Faraday cage', never mind know what it means or how to make one. You cannot possibly have been working alone. You must have had help. So tell me, who else knows about me and Paul?"

Adam didn't speak.

"Cat got your tongue, huh? Well, I think I might be able to find a way to loosen your lips."

"If you're so smart, Fillmore, why don't you tell me what I should have done instead?"

"What is this, a Batman episode? Where the villain gets up on his soapbox and gloats while the heroes plot their escape? Well, why not? You're not going anywhere, and Paul's in no condition to do much of anything. Are you, Paul?"

Paul suddenly found himself in charge of his voice. "Adam, I'm so sorry. I can't..."

Abruptly he was cut off and Fillmore took over again.

"Your problem, Adam, is that you're about twenty years behind me in terms of technology. You're like a caveman trying to understand a microprocessor. It could never work. The only way you can beat my software is with better software, and you just don't have the capability to do it.

"You want to know what you should have done? OK, I'll tell you. It's a shame you're not where I am, Adam. My real body is sitting here in my den, where there is a much more elegant solution to your problem. If you were here, you'd be able to issue the shutdown command, and the nanos in Paul's body would simply detach themselves from his nerves and quietly turn themselves off. Then they would be nothing more than inert molecule-sized dust that would get cleaned up by Paul's body's normal processes. He'd pee grey for a few days and be completely fine."

Fillmore leaned down over Adam's taut body and leered in his face.

"Here, I've even got it called up on my screen. The command can only be issued manually; it can't be triggered from my own net. Wouldn't want to fire it accidentally, you know. One little keypress would do the trick. Can you press the 'enter' key from where you are, Adam? Hmm? Go ahead, try. Try."

Adam seethed.

"You're pathetic," said Fillmore, turning to the tray of hot skewers.

Anne Marie slipped silently away from the top of the basement steps and headed toward the front door. Before leaving, she whispered instructions to Adam's house system to wait one minute, then call her mobile. She wasn't sure how well sounds would travel up the basement steps to the audio pickup upstairs, but she didn't want to be totally cut off from what was happening.

She ran to her car and gave the nav system the address of Fillmore's house. It turned out to be fairly close by; the nav system estimated the trip would take fourteen minutes under normal conditions. She vowed to make it in half that.

The mobile chirped. She picked up and immediately turned on the mute so that she could hear but not be heard. The only sounds that came out of the speaker were indistinct. They could have been muffled voices or just static.

Driving down the narrow streets, she had time to second-guess herself. The MRI plan had been the best that she and Adam could come up with. She had had reservations about it from the beginning, mainly because it would take too long. Ideally, she wanted to knock Fillmore out of Paul's life with one sudden stroke. Anything less left the slimy worm too much opportunity to fight back. But no one they had consulted could suggest anything like that - in fact, no one took them seriously enough to consider it more than a hypothetical situation - and so the MRI idea had seemed like their best chance.

Now, though, fate had presented her with a better opportunity. She just hoped Adam wouldn't suffer too badly while she crawled through traffic.

Adam hissed as the hot metal made contact with his skin. He squirmed in his bonds, but there was no slack at all. Fillmore compensated easily for his small movements, and soon the first of the barbs had been inserted into Adam's chest. It went in horizontally just below his collarbone, parallel to his shoulders about halfway between the midline of his chest and his right nipple. Fillmore worked it in further, just underneath the skin, until the tip poked out again another inch to the right. Adam stopped trying to move then, not wanting to shake the skewer and cause himself more damage. At least the shaft was thin - there wasn't enough metal to hold the heat for long and it had already cooled off considerably.

"There we go," Fillmore said when he was satisfied with the positioning. "Now let's open you up, my little sardine can."

He took the utility knife and made a thin incision over the top of the barb, then made two starter cuts in parallel lines straight down from the points where the barb passed through Adam's skin. He grasped the shaft and slowly began to turn it. Adam's skin began to tear away from the tissue beneath in an inch-wide strip that steadily progressed down his chest.

Adam's already tense muscles tightened even more up and down the length of his stretched-out body. His breath caught in his throat for a long time. Then he let out a thin, high-pitched scream.

"Turn, damn it!" shouted Anne Marie at the traffic light. The streets were not as congested at this hour as they would have been earlier in the evening, but there was still enough oncoming traffic that she couldn't just jump the light. Her ears were still ringing. She had had the volume cranked up, straining to listen through the fuzzy static for anything that Fillmore and Adam might be saying, and when the screaming had started, it was deafening. She quickly damped down the sound, but disturbing though it was, she couldn't bring herself to turn it off completely.

It suddenly dawned on her that, whatever their reasons had been for not involving the authorities before, circumstances had now changed. She put the call from Adam's house on hold and linked to 911. They picked up at once.

"I need you to send an ambulance to this address," Anne Marie said. "You'll find one, possibly two men in need of medical help. Do you think you can be there in under five minutes? No? That's fine. Oh, and I also need some cops here." She gave them Fillmore's street number, then broke the link. The sound of Adam's screaming resumed.

"Hang in there, Adam. Five minutes is all I need," she muttered as the light finally changed and she slammed across the intersection.

Three strips of flesh now hung in wet curls at the base of Adam's belly. His breathing was heavy and ragged. Fillmore sat back and took a break.

"Feel like telling me who you're working with yet? No? OK, I've got all night."

He stretched his arms over his head and cracked Paul's knuckles.

"I wish I could claim I was doing this for some greater good, Adam, but the truth is, I'm not," he said. "I'm just doing it because it turns me on. Come on, now, answer me honestly. All the talk about S&M play having to be 'safe, sane, and consensual' is just a bunch of hooey, don't you think? If our roles were reversed and you had an opportunity like this, wouldn't you take advantage of it?"

"No," Adam gasped. "No, I wouldn't."

"Why not? Don't have the guts?" sneered Fillmore.

"That's not why. You're a sick, amoral bastard and because of that, you assume everyone else is too. But you're wrong. S&M is not about causing unwanted pain. It's about people agreeing to explore each others' bodies and interests. Without that agreement, it's not S&M, it's just torture."

"Ah, semantics," said Fillmore.

"It's not semantics, it makes all the difference in the world. I only tie up guys who want to be tied up. I only whip the backs of guys who want to be whipped. I only have sex with guys who want to have sex with me. And the reason I don't go further than that is not because I don't have the guts, but because *it's wrong!*" He stopped, drained by the effort of speech.

"I don't buy it," said Fillmore. "Right and wrong are just arbitrary concepts. They don't have any meaning in and of themselves. They only have meaning because society decides they do. And in case you've been asleep for a decade or two, society is very different today than it used to be.

"We aren't organized in tribe-like geographically-based communities any more. Technology has split us into a zillion tiny groups that share common interests but usually have nothing in common physically. Each one of those groups sets its own rules for its members and makes its own decisions about 'right' and 'wrong'. And whoever has the best technology controls the discussion. Right now, we three have a little community of our own. I control the technology - and let's be honest, you two are like Stone Age primitives compared with me - thus, I decide what's right and what's wrong.

"It's all about the technology these days. You're either in control of the system, or the system is in control of you. You guys are living in the past, but not me. I've got the tech, and that's what matters. It's all about the tech."

He paused in his oration, seeming to realize that he was

pontificating.

"You know what, Adam, this whole discussion is getting tedious. I liked you better when you were screaming." He reached to pick up another skewer, then suddenly froze and said "What? Oh, shit."

Paul's body collapsed like a deflating balloon, then lay still and lifeless on the floor.

For Paul, the horror just kept growing. He had watched helplessly as his own body committed acts of unspeakable torment on the man who had been his last hope of escape. He had boiled in impotent fury at his own helplessness to be more than a passive observer. He had wailed at the injustice, that this man who was barely more than a stranger to him had tried to help him and was now being rewarded with agony and impending death, all at his own hands.

Then, with no warning, the world went away.

It was just like the previous time. There was no light, no sound, no sensation of any kind. He could not feel his limbs, or the thudding of his heart in his chest, or the pull of the earth. He had no muscles, no bones, no eyes or ears, nothing.

There was nothing at all except the frantic racing of his own thoughts in their dark, silent prison.

And for all he knew, it might last forever this time.

"It's all about the tech." Paul's flat, nasal voice crackled from the mobile at her waist.

Anne Marie poked the tip of the wooden baseball bat through the glass door and it gave way with a satisfying crash. She reached in through the hole she had made and turned the knob. The house alarm sounded, filling the air with a shrill whistle. From the mobile she heard Paul's voice say "What? Oh, shit."

She stalked down the unlit hall and turned to find Fillmore sitting bathed in the blue-green glow of his electronics. He was clearly disoriented, no doubt surprised to be pulled away from Paul's body to deal with an unexpected emergency in his own. She stormed across the rubble-covered floor of the room, covering the distance in three long strides.

Fillmore spoke as he worked to untangle himself, his voice nasal and whiny. "Well, if it isn't the little chiquita. I suppose you're here to talk about..."

His voice cut off abruptly when the bat swung into the side of his head. Tangled in wires and slouched in his chair he had no chance of avoiding the blow. His body swung to the side and toppled over onto the floor.

"Guess again," said Anne Marie.

She bent down over the still form. A thin stream of blood began to trickle from his ear. She couldn't tell if he was breathing or not. "I find that oftentimes the low-tech solution works best," Anne Marie muttered. She took careful aim and slammed the bat once more into his skull.

This time he definitely wasn't breathing. She stepped over to the console screen. It glowed brightly in the dark room. Numerous windows and icons covered the screen, with graphs and meters flickering in ever-changing displays. One window, though, was a basic console, the kind hackers had preferred ever since the first TTY machines at the dawn of the information age. Pale grey text sat static against a black background. The text was gibberish to Anne Marie, but she had no doubt that the cryptic letters spelled out the shutdown command Fillmore had taunted Adam with.

The only question was, was shutting down Paul's nerve net all it would do? Or would it also trigger the heart attack Fillmore had spoken of?

Anne Marie spoke under her breath. "You can dither for hours, or days, or even years. But in the end, you just have to act."

She pressed 'enter'.

Perception came back slowly, not all in a rush the way it had the last time. Paul first felt a tingle in his right index finger, though he could feel nothing at all of the arm and hand between it and his brain. Then he felt a tremendous spasm in his left calf. A wash of staticky noise burst in his ears, then vanished again.

Slowly, painfully, light and sound and sensations returned to Paul's body. He didn't even try to move as it happened, overwhelmed by the jumble of mixed messages coming in through his nervous system. The air moving through the ventilation system sounded dark green; the pressure of the floor under his body tasted like butter; the flickering light of the candle flames dancing against the wall smelled like carrots, then sewage, then lilacs. He lay on the floor and waited for the world to start making sense again.

At last, he became aware that one of the sounds he was hearing was his name. "Paul? Paul? Come on, Paul, come back."

He tried to move his legs, fully expecting them to not respond, but to his surprise, they did. Somewhat shakily, he climbed to his feet and moved over to Adam's racked body.

"Paul, is that you?" Adam asked. The wounds on his chest were raw and red, seeping blood and pale fluid down his sides and onto the table and floor.

"Yes," Paul answered, a trace of wonder in his voice. "Yes, it's me. For now, at least."

Then he shook himself together and set to work unchaining Adam's wrists. "I don't know how long this will last, but I'm going to make good use of whatever time I've got."

They made it upstairs just as the paramedics arrived at the door.

The gathering at the Minherden Gallery Of Modern Art was not a capacity crowd, but Anne Marie was gratified all the same at the number of people who had turned out for the exhibit. In the two years since she had left her high-paying but very frustrating managerial job, her art had blossomed. It had taken a lot of urging from Paul and from her friends, but at last she had agreed to do submit her work to the gallery.

They liked it enough to give her three rooms - smallish ones, but adequate - and some publicity, and now here she was, surrounded by friends, family, colleagues, and even some complete strangers, all of whom had come to see her work. It was wonderful, but deep down Anne Marie was still in a state of disbelief. There was no way she could possibly deserve this kind of recognition.

Paul clearly felt otherwise. He could not stop praising her accomplishments to anyone and everyone who would listen. He was currently bending the ears of the Thamphutragashes, an elderly couple who had been on the museum's board since before Anne Marie was born. She couldn't make out the words, but she had a good idea of what they were talking about. Embarrassing though the lavish accolades sometimes were, his unwavering support of her reminded her once again how lucky she was to have met and married the perfect man. And how lucky she was not to have lost him...

"Congratulations, Anne Marie!"

She turned from her brief reverie to see Adam and his partner Wayne, their hands occupied with plates of hors d'oeuvres and glasses of Merlot. "Adam! Wayne! So glad you could come," she said.

"I wouldn't have missed this," said Adam. "Your big night." He paused to take a bite of baked brie. "You know that we all miss you terribly back at the office, but this was the smartest career move you could have made. You've got a gift, Anne Marie. You were just wasting it making ads for mouthwash and peanut butter."

"You're sweet," she said.

"I'm sincere," he replied. "Where's Paul?"

"Schmoozing, as usual." She gestured with her glass over to where Paul was standing.

"Did he decide to get that work done yet?"

They both knew what work he was referring to. The whip marks all over Paul's back were the only physical reminder of the time he had spent in Fillmore's captivity. Cosmetic surgery could have made the ridges and lines less obvious, but the only way to restore his skin to its original condition was to use nanotech. Tiny machines would stimulate his cells to repair the damage in a way that conventional medicine could not. Paul, however, was apprehensive at the thought of more nanomachines crawling around in his body.

"Almost," said Anne Marie. "He wants to get rid of the marks but the problem is, in his mind, the cure is worse than the scars."

"That's understandable," said Wayne. "I can't blame him."

"It works, though," said Adam. "I'd offer to show you my flawless chest as proof, but this just isn't the right time and place."

"Oh, I disagree," said Wayne, leering. "This is the perfect time to show me your flawless chest."

"Good grief," said Anne Marie, turning her back.

"Hey, you haven't had any more legal trouble, have you?" asked Adam.

"No, thank God," she replied. "For a week or so there was some debate over whether they were going to charge me in Fillmore's death, but they didn't. Which is good, because it was a clear case of self-defense."

"Or spouse defense," said Adam.

Anne Marie turned to greet a trio of well-wishers, exchanging the pleasantries that had become automatic over the course of the evening.

"In a way it's a shame the slimeball died," said Wayne when the trio had moved on. "Then he would have been the one facing charges."

"Not at all," answered Anne Marie. "I try not to even think about what might have happened if he had survived."

"What do you mean?" asked Wayne.

"Well, consider this," said Anne Marie. "Fillmore was unusual for a hacker type. Most of those guys make a breakthrough - a virus or worm or a slammer, whatever it is - and post it immediately on the net, where thousands of copycats start refining variants of the original code. Fillmore didn't share his ideas with anyone, and he used very secure encryption to protect the files on his computers. Can you imagine what would have happened if Fillmore had been less paranoid?

"Think of what the military could do with his technology. Why train an expensive soldier to do a job only to have him get killed doing it? Far more cost-effective to train the soldier then send a convict or a junkie or some other socially undesirable person into harm's way by remote control. For that matter, any boring or dangerous task could be automated. Any job that is too sophisticated for a robot but too repetitive and dull to stimulate a human mind would be fair game. Just get someone to perform the task once, then replay the action over and over again for an eight-hour shift. And I don't want to even imagine what another psychopath like Fillmore might come up with.

"Now, as far as I know, no one has been able to crack Fillmore's encryption. I pray that there was some kind of self-destruct on the data and that it's irretrievably lost by now, but I'll never know for sure. But if Fillmore had lived, it would have been a different story. I have no doubt that the CIA or the NSA would have swooped in and spirited him away under some bureaucratic double-speak to something that was called 'custody' but was actually a lab with all the tools he needed for more development work. Thank God, that couldn't happen."

"Are you sure?" asked Wayne.

"What do you mean?"

"I mean, are you sure he's dead?"

"He wasn't breathing. I checked."

"He had a nanonet running parallel to his nervous system just like Paul, didn't he? Nanomachines don't need oxygen. They could have repaired any damage to his cells while he was 'dead'..."

There was a long silence while the implications sank in.

Anne Marie took a slow sip from her wine. "That's a very scary thought, but I've got a scarier one," she said. "Even if you're right and Fillmore is still alive and working, it's been more than three years and he hasn't bothered us yet. The real problem is this: the genie is out of the bottle. Now that what he did is known to be possible, inevitably someone will figure out how he did it. One of these days, someone somewhere is going to reproduce his work. Then God only knows what will happen.

She took another long drink. "That's my big fear. That's what keeps me awake at night."

Neither Adam nor Wayne could think of anything to say.

Paul returned then, a bundle of energy and enthusiasm. He stopped short upon seeing the seriousness of their expressions. "Whoa, come on guys, this is a party. Why the long faces?"

Adam turned to face Paul and put his hands on his shoulders. "Well, my friend," he said, "we were just discussing what an enormous, gigantic, titanic, colossal..." He punctuated each adjective with a squeeze to the meat under his fingers. "... utter *tragedy* it is that this fabulous body of yours is being wasted on a woman. No offense, Anne Marie," he said over his shoulder.

"None taken," Anne Marie said lightly.

"You know, of course, that if you ever want to shake the cloying conventionality of heterosexualism, all you have to do is say the word and Wayne and I will be more than happy to provide you with an escort on your journey of self-discovery."

Paul stood frozen for a moment. "I do believe that under all those fancy words, you're hitting on me."

Adam just stared into Paul's eyes.

"Well, the old Paul would not have taken that well, but I'm a changed man," said Paul. He raised his own arms up inside Adam's to put his hands on Adam's shoulders. "I certainly do owe you - you did save my life, after all. And since you bring up the subject, I have to confess that you were an... exquisite lover. Rough and fierce, yet surprisingly tender and sensitive. Not at all what I had expected. Really, the best that any man could ask for."

Wayne and Anne Marie exchanged glances with their eyebrows raised.

"But I'm married, and you've got Wayne. It just wouldn't be fair to either of our significant others if I were to accept your offer, tempting though it may be. So I'll tell you what - you work it out with the two of them and get back to me."

Paul moved his hands to the back of Adam's head, pulled him forward, and planted a long kiss on Adam's lips. Then he slapped him twice gently on the cheek and walked across the room to greet a trio of Anne Marie's admirers who had just come in.

Wayne, Adam, and Anne Marie watched him go, blinking and trying to decide whether to be stunned or to burst out laughing. Wayne cracked first. The others followed only seconds later. Soon all three were snorting and hiccuping and hoping none of the splashing Merlot was landing on their clothes.

Adam was the first to recover to the point where he could speak. "Well, that answers that," he said. "Obviously, he's still possessed."

Mind Games

A Boner Book

About the Author

Alan DiLuca writes software for a living and occasionally dabbles in gay bondage fiction. He loves maps, languages, quantum physics, the clarinet, and watching - or being - a man struggling in tightly tied ropes. He lives in Bethlehem, Pennsylvania, with his husband of thirteen years.